Foreword

This book, "*God in the Marketplace,*" is spiritually-based. It seeks to relate God and the everyday business world. The main theme throughout is the writers "hearing the voice of God within" and demonstrates how a world-class business enterprise resulted from the "hearing" to the "doing." The book is the sequel to an earlier book, *Speak-To-It!*

Table of Contents

Preface 2
Introduction. 8
Chapter I "I told you 'No!'" 24
Chapter II "I want you to return to Georgia" 28
Chapter III "If I don't come back on that date you must seek Me for a whole new view of Eschatology!" 31
Chapter IV "I'll show the world what I will do!" . . . 42
Chapter V "A Rhema Word" 50
Chapter VI "You must seek Me for a whole new view of everything!" 54
Chapter VII "What concerns you?" 75
Chapter VIII "Write it down!" 79
Chapter IX "Jarrell is going to give you that land!" . 86
Chapter X A Couple of Other Times God Spoke . . . 89
Chapter XI A New Awareness Emerging 93
Addendum I New Insights Gained from Listening . . . 97
Addendum II The Republican National Convention . . 102
Addendum III Secrets of Success 115
How To Listen 120
Key Vocabulary Words. 126

Preface

In this book I am testifying to when God spoke to me, which I feel is the most important issue facing Christians, and the world. It is a *right now* issue, relevant to our crucial time in history (our survival is at stake), relating to world terrorism all the way to our going to the grocery store to buy a jar of peanut butter!

Since it is my own testimony, it is extremely personal. I am sharing what I heard God say to me. It is, therefore, an intimate account of God (or Spirit) speaking to my spirit. It is not an academic treatise, for that is not the way God speaks. He speaks to your inner spirit within, no outside voices from the sky.

Testimony

The key word in this essay is "TESTIMONY." That is, what happened to me — not what happened to someone else, though there are many accounts of God talking to others. The Bible is full of it.

I am reminded of what C.B. Carter said to a group in North Carolina a couple of years back when he told them, "I'm tired of hearing what God said to Moses, Isaiah, Jeremiah, David, or Paul ... I want to hear what God told YOU! What has God told you?"

This, I am told, stunned the audience and the response was one of silence!

Then C.B. challenged them, "Why don't you lay the Bible down and listen to God for yourself?" After considerable discussion he softened his "blows" by saying they should "take the Bible up again!"

C.B. became an instant hero to me. I think he put his finger right on the issue of our times — hearing God for ourselves! The Bible certainly has my greatest respect as a "portion" of God's Word. But it does not contain everything God has said or is "saying to the churches" — to you and me!

You see, most of us have heard very little, if any, teaching of God speaking directly to us. Usually when one says "God told me" it is a sure sign that he is either a lunatic or "off the wall!" Now I am positive that this is often the case but I am convinced that we need to hear afresh (now) from God in this crucial present moment.

Regarding the word "testimony," I really think that this has replaced great preaching! As a theologian and preacher, I was taught that to communicate God to man, I had to wrestle one hour of study for one minute of preaching. There wasn't much emphasis in listening to what God is saying. Rather than that church-goers on Sundays hearing "THUS SAITH THE LORD," it was some theological discourse dug out of boring research. No wonder the listeners went to sleep! I even heard of one preacher who yawned in his own sermon. And, it seemed that the more educated the speaker was, the more boring he came across — the "Ph.D" more than the man with the bachelors degree. Well, let's get off this before I turn off all the doctors — but remember, I am one myself!

I think in this area of "testimony" the Mormons exemplify greatly what I am saying. I watch the Mormon channel (BYU-TV) at my home and you hear almost no preaching, but you hear plenty of "testimonies!" This may account, partially, for their rapid growth throughout the world.

Real Life

In this little book, I am simply "reporting" eight or ten real-life experiences of what I perceived was God speaking to me. Sometimes it was questions, sometimes, answers. On occasion is was a dialogue between God and me. I was thinking just this morning, "What if I had not heard God speak, paid no attention, or worse, did not follow after directions I was given?" You see, this matter of God speaking is not just some "preacher-in-the-sky"

(God) pontificating — it is practical! Where the rubber meets the road. On occasion it might even save someone's life. The point of this book is that *we'd better be listening!*

Toward the end, I will attempt a little analysis of what I heard ... but this is not to say we can analyze God.

Throughout this little book I will mention a few names and a little humor — for some of what God says is funny! Rather than being the pompous-faced, stereotyped preacher we have known, stern, solemn, serious, holy tones ... I have discovered that God even laughs! Out loud! Or so it seems. I am convinced He invented laughter and lightheartedness — all within the scope of what he called "JOY!" Oh, pardon me, that's what he told someone else, the Apostle Paul.

Doughton Park

I am beginning this manuscript at Doughton Park, N.C., on the Blue Ridge Parkway. I just finished breakfast: country ham, red-eye gravy, biscuits, an egg, sorghum and coffee. All this was prepared by Edna, my wife of 54 years. The wind is blowing. The sun is shining. It is 63 degrees. It is quiet. I've heard several sounds of nature. What a place for inspiration (in-SPIRIT-ation). It seems like I am hearing — right now — God speaking. Anyhow, the thoughts are coming, rapidly, faster than I can write. (I hope Keli, my helper in preparing the manuscript, can read it!)

A word about how small the world is. Upon parking our motorhome yesterday afternoon, the very first people I met know my lifetime friend, Crosby Few, an attorney who lives and practices in Tampa, Fla. In fact, they were related by marriage to him. The last time I think I saw Crosby was when he was singing a solo *"I Am So Glad That Our Father in Heaven"* when he was but a teenager at the old First Methodist Church in New Smyrna Beach, Fla.

The very next couple, the Morgans, parked adjacent to us, knew Charlie Vaughan and Bill Blomely, both living back in Ellijay, Ga., my hometown for the last 15 years.

Finally, I will conclude this writing by offering some clues or suggestions of how you might consider hearing or listening to the voice of God within.

I would surely like to hear from you as to what He says!

Please write to:

> Col. Oscar Poole
> P.O. Box 690
> East Ellijay, GA 30539

P.S. My earlier book, *Speak-To-It!* (2004), is available upon request, as well as my musical CD of piano playing, *Col. Poole's Favorites*, played at the world-famous Col.

Poole's BAR-B-Q and in mini-concerts around the country.

Further note: While I have heard the voice of God many times in my lifetime of 74 years, the times mentioned in his book have occurred since 1985 to the present. His voice is more frequent now that I have "tuned in" or have begun to focus on listening.

It was out of this "hearing from God (the voice within)," that our world-famous business enterprise developed — Col. Poole's Georgia BAR-B-Q. Hence, the title of this book, *God in the Marketplace*.

Introduction

While eating a meal in a restaurant about four years ago, a friend told me that he had never heard the voice of God — "in fact," he told me, "God does not speak today." I replied to him that I was sure God had spoken to him many times, but he had not been listening.

So we got into quite a conversation. The religious group to which he belonged told him that God quit speaking at the close of the first century A.D. — that upon the completion of the New Testament, God ceased talking to man. That if you want to "hear" God you must read what God said to someone else. Let me say up front that my response to this idea is "BALONEY!" I think this is silly and ridiculous, even stupid, not that anyone who believes this way is stupid. I do not cease to be amazed at the numbers of people whose appearance seems to be of a high culture and sophistication that accept such primitive belief systems!

Before going any further I ask the reader to not only hear me out but to "think" me out! Then, if you do not believe that God speaks today, or if you are not hearing God directly for yourself — let's still be friends.

Back to the conversation with my friend.

I shared with him how God spoke directly into my inner spirit about placing my BAR-B-Q restaurant "over on that hill." (One of the most significant times I have heard God speak in my life — covered in a later chapter.)

"Well," he said, "God never talked to me!"

I asked him if God was tongue-tied, did He not want to, or could not or just would not?! I asked him if he knew the hymn *"In the Garden"* from which I sang to him the part that says *"And He walks with me and He talks with me, and He tells me I am His own."*

"Oh Yes," he said, "We sing it often."

I replied that he should not sing it again — "Why should you sing something you do not believe?!" I found myself pontificating (preaching) just a little. I told him I thought this was hypocritical — saying one thing and doing the opposite. Added to this, I think it is double-talk.

To deny that God speaks actively today is to deny that God is God! In effect, if we believe that we are placing ourselves superior to God. We can do something that He cannot do!

You mean the inventor of words can't talk or does not talk, especially today — right now — when we need to hear a new message?

If God does not speak today then is He playing

favorites — that is, He spoke with the first century Christians, but not to us? Would that even be moral?

At the very least, this view is some kind of DEISM — that God moved to some distant place and left us to ourselves. For example, if one wanted to know something he would have to consult what God told somebody else at a different time and in a different place under different circumstances, about different issues and subjects?

No! A thousand times no! That's not the way it is. God is personally active and involved in the affairs of earth — RIGHT NOW! And much if not most, is in speaking directly into the hearts of men who will listen, without Bible references or third party interpreters of what was said long ago!

To say that God quit speaking makes God boring and irrelevant. That's why much of what goes on inside today's churches is such.

This denies creativity. There would never be any thing new. We'd be plowing corn behind mules with sticks. We'd have no art, nor artists, no great literature, no William Shakespeares, no poets. To maintain God does not speak denies inspiration itself. No inspiring hymns or dramas, no music. No moving cantatas, no musicals. We'd all go around repeating over and over what somebody else said, having no relevance to our lives today. Ho hum! Te dum! Dumb-dumb! No life. No fresh ideas. Just old dead crumbs instead of fresh manna from above!

Before you confine God speaking to "The Word" — meaning the canon of the 66 books comprising both the old and new testaments — consider an insight I received from Des Walter a few days ago (Des is a traveling seminar speaker from Australia who spends a couple of months each year in America).

Des said that the Bible as we know it today, was denied to all people, except a few monks holed up in monasteries, for the first 1,700 years! So according to the fundamentalist, all persons preceding our generation were simply "out of luck!"

Let me illustrate how some Christians go about making life's decisions, going places and doing things. Some, even people I know, unless they can find some Bible verse or scripture reference to back up or affirm their decisions and actions, don't make any new moves. Hence, they remain in their "comfort zones" and never move out beyond their little worlds, threatened by every whim of adversity, thence never amount to or accomplish much. All the while "thumping their Bibles," judging everyone else, as "evil." Well, that being true, I belong to such an "evil" category!

So far I am sort of contrasting the two opposite views of the "God quit speaking at the close of the first century" group, to the "God is speaking now" group (of which I am a part).

As I said earlier, I think this God-speaking issue is

probably the most crucial of our times. Simply stated, we'll never make it through the 21st century with the old worn-out cliches and techniques of the old systems, well intended or not.

Hearing, But Not Hearing

Isaiah the prophet said that the heart of the people was "fat," that they could not hear. *"Seeing, they see not; and hearing, they hear not."* Jesus spoke the same theme about the people of his day. We have much of this today amongst organized religion. People attend church and hear words, but not *The Word*. To many the Bible is simply what God told someone else and many have never been able to "relate" wordy sermons to real life. They hear with their physical ears but not their hearts. They hear intellectually, but not spiritually. They hear with their heads, but not with their hearts, and then when occasionally one hears what is said in churches it is, as I said, what God told someone else.

The essence of this little book is that God speaks directly to everyone — in church and out of church. If only we will listen we can hear Him speak everywhere, in our homes, places of worship, while traveling, awake or sleeping — anywhere and everywhere in every conceivable manner! Whispers. In silence mostly. In situations. Circumstances. Problems. God speaks in the whirlwind.

The storm. The twilight. The night. He speaks in and through dreams. He speaks when our spirits are lighthearted or heavy and depressed. He speaks most loudly in "the still, small voice!" But speak He does and it behooves us to learn to listen!

When Jesus was about to leave His disciples, He told them "I'm going away, I will send the Holy Spirit to you. He will testify of me. He will comfort you. He will guide you. He will show you things to come. He will teach you!"

Now pray tell me — how does the Holy Spirit do this without speaking or talking in intelligible words that we can understand? But some will say this all quit when the apostles died! Who says?

The Apostle John declared, "You have an anointing (another word for Christ) within. You have no need that any man should teach you!" This means that you have within you *The Christ* and He teaches (speaks to you). And this was long before anyone had a Bible — even before much of it was written!

In Rev. 3:20 it is clear that God speaks to His people. *"If any man HEAR MY VOICE..."* I would suppose that for one to hear there must be One to speak!

Asking — Answering

In another place the scriptures declare, *"If any man*

lacks wisdom let him ASK." Again, I would suppose that when one asks, God is there to answer!

This hints of a dialogue, a conversation between God and man. In a couple of hearing situations that follow, it was just that — a conversation between God and me. We talked with each other!

So if you have a question; ask!

Biblical

I'm sure that the reader has picked up by now that I am saying that God speaks outside the Bible! That is absolutely correct. The Bible is what God told *them* — outside the Bible is what God tells *you*!

Does this in any way "put down" the Bible? No! The Bible is God's Word — but so is what He speaks to you! On the same level? Of course whenever God speaks — it does not matter in what form — it's still God's word.

When God speaks through a different source than the Bible, it is still biblical! God spoke directly to Jeremiah — God speaks directly to you. That's biblical, too! If God tells you to go to 445 Center Street in a certain city — that's God's word! This idea that God ONLY speaks through the canonized books contained in the Holy Scriptures makes God a relic instead of a relevant God. God is the SAME yesterday, TODAY and FOREVER! If He talked then, He talks now! God is a personal God —

and persons speak. Nowhere in the Bible is it said that God quit speaking — EVER — and if it does not say it, no one has that authority!

Logos — Rhema

Now does God speak to you through the Bible? Absolutely! When the Spirit within you "brings to life" a certain scripture, that is called a *rhema* word. There is a whole school on this in Oklahoma. The written word is called *logos*. So, when the logos word is "made alive" to you we speak of it as rhema word. This has happened to me on many occasions, but I wonder how many times I have missed hearing from God directly for myself because of my almost total focus on Bible stories and references as has been the tradition passed down to us by our elders.

I need to assert again that the testimonies given in this booklet are not meant to take away from this rhema discussion. In fact, it comes to me as I am writing this, that it might be impossible to separate the direct voice of God from what we call a "rhema event." The moment the Spirit makes alive a written word one begins to see images and word-phrases that are associated in our minds, which have become spiritually activated.

A good example of this is when the Spirit within me "activated" Rev. 12:11, which is forthcoming in this book. You will note, therefore, that Gods speaking to me has been both directly and through a rhema word.

You see, we must not limit or confine God to the Bible or any book for that matter. I must admit that the testimonies I am about to give caught me off guard and by surprise! But I am saying they should not have. Like many Christians I was conditioned to hearing God via a third party and not for myself. Since hearing from God so dramatically and clearly and with subsequent results I have come to recondition myself to the possibility of hearing God's voice.

So, you can see there has been a CHANGE for me in this whole area of listening — hearing. The "eyes of my understanding" have been opened and I am experiencing many changes in my spiritual growth. This brings me to a brief discussion of progressive revelation.

Progressive Revelation

Our journey-of-faith needs to be seen as progressive — a journey always moving and *"changing from glory to glory"* (2 Cor. 3:18). While God and truth are eternal constants and never change, our understanding and perceptions are always changing. Or at least, they should be! That is what's wrong with most of Christendom as far as I am concerned.

History is replete with one major change after

another. God gives a new revelation to one generation, then another, then another. It seems that each time God reveals Himself in a NEW way those who are affected by it decide to "camp" around the new doctrine, teaching or experience, become bogged down and refuse to move forward. Then when God moves in another new direction the past "new" folks become the "old" folks, contention sets in and the "old" tries to destroy the "new." The cycle is again repeated until this scenario happens repeatedly. This, in my opinion, has been our sad lot and heritage.

Am I contending to "throw out" all the "old?" Absolutely not! Keep the good in the old, throw out the tired, useless, dead traditions and embrace the good of the NEW. Continue this until the goal is reached: the "one new man in Christ" that Paul talks about in Ephesians 4.

Tree of Good and Evil

It has just dawned upon me that the above discussion sounds a little like partaking of the tree of "the knowledge of good and evil." I want to try to clear this up. I certainly do not want to create the impression that we are to mix good with evil. And I know there will be some reading this who only see the good. I have tried to do this myself. But somehow, someway, there is evil to be dealt with. *"Woe to him who calls good evil and who calls evil good"* (Isaiah 5:20). Also, we are to discern between the two. We are not to mix the two, good and evil, but to separate the two and run from the *"very appearance of evil"* (1 Thess. 5:22). I believe this to be true, no matter how you define evil — as "darkness" or "the mere absence of light," or whatever. This is not a treatise on good and evil — I'll leave that to someone else whose understanding may be closer to the truth than mine. This is just a thought or two that sprang forth in the above discussion regarding dealing with our pilgrim journeys of moving forward from the old into the new. I suppose I want to say let us have a profound respect for the old, keeping some of it (this decision arrived at by an inner awareness and revelation) and moving into the new with the same profound respect. Let us not be afraid of change, though it is natural to do so.

Individual and Collective

I think all of the above needs to be arrived at individually — one at a time. But we are all connected by virtue of what we are — children of God! As new revelations of TRUTH are discovered (it's coming faster these days and often simultaneously) the new awareness moves from a few individuals into a group, keeps expanding into a "collective consciousness." You see, God has a goal for the *"knowledge of God to cover the earth as the waters cover the sea"* (Habakkuk 2:14, Isaiah 11:9). Also, that *"everyone should know Him from the least to the greatest"* (Jeremiah 31:34). His plan is for peace and good will for all men. This is what is going on amongst us and will not and cannot be stopped! This in spite of obstacles and threats of terrorism and the very threat of annihilation.

As I am trying to move from this discussion to sharing the significant times God has spoken to me, let me repeat that rather than a "return to the old," let us move toward that which is NEW — for *"Behold, I make all things new"* (Rev. 21:5). And remember that all we have is right now — the *eternal now!*

A Further Word About Progressive Revelation

I am sure that some will read this material and not understand what I mean when I say "progressive revelation." One way to say this is that there are many understandings of truth today unknown by our forebears. This is no discredit to any of them. Ten years or so from now there will be newer discoveries of truth and what is new now will become old. It's like computers. You buy one, and only three months later it is out of date. So, we must stay on our toes, so to speak. While some of this new stuff is threatening, it is also exciting and adventuresome! So, come on and let the wind blow in your face!

Thought Connections

These next few thoughts may seem like a little diversion from our topic of when God spoke to me, but after a brief nap I think I see a "connection." From time to time Edna and I meet some of the nicest people on our travels and I want to share with you two of them that we met just last year, here at Doughton Park, N.C.

They are Ralph and Gerri Templeton, from Statesville, N.C. Our acquaintance with them began right here where I am writing this material, 14 months ago in May '03. Upon meeting them we immediately bonded and connected with them. In fact, we "fell in love with them!" Throughout the year Ralph has e-mailed me occasionally and we have talked on the phone a time or two.

Anyhow, a great relationship continues with Ralph and Gerri. These are wonderful people — our kind. Edna and I love to BE with them! Not that it matters, but these are prestigious people. They were members of the world-famed Calvary Church in Charlotte, N.C., where Billy Graham, Bev Shea and T. W. Wilson often attended. I think Ralph was a former Sunday School Superintendent there. On one occasion Ralph shared with me that he and Billy Graham spoke on the same program!

Ralph and Gerri experienced the loss of one of their daughters in a tragic fire some years ago. This they shared with Edna and me last year. But instead of becoming bitter and resentful at God, they are two of the kindest and most tender, loving persons we have met. Ralph and Gerri work with an organization called "The Compassionate Friends," a group that counsels with and lends support to persons who have lost children and helps them to work through their grief.

Thoughts

But why am I mentioning them? What connection, if any, do they have with hearing — listening? While taking a brief nap it seemed to be revealed to me.

Just five days ago, while passing by Statesville where they live, I thought about them. (I deal with "thoughts" in my previous book, *Speak-To-It*.)

On Sunday, while visiting with Gary and Carol Sigler, I said to Edna, "Maybe we ought to call Ralph and Gerri and have them meet us atop the Blue Ridge Parkway." Then we sort of passed it off — that they might be busy and I need some quality time in the writing of this book. I mentioned them again during the day. Then again the next day — Monday when we left for this place.

The next day (Tuesday) I was standing in the driveway when ... want to guess who drove by in their RV? Ralph and Gerri! I wasn't sure at first, but I kept looking. "That looks like Ralph's profile!" They stopped. We ran over. It WAS them! Ralph and Gerri!

I experienced a chill down my spine. We had been talking and thinking about them for three days, and there they were.

Did they pick up on our thoughts? Or we theirs?! This is just what I had been "thinking" about for several weeks — that we communicate even with our thought life! Our thoughts reach out unto the universe — search for answers — much like a search engine on a computer — and return back to us!

A few experiences like this and you will begin to believe there is something to what I am trying to say!

A connection to this book's topic? Then what is it? You see, prayer is communication. Speaking. Requesting. Asking. Responding.

It looks like our thoughts are a part of the same! We think a thought — another picks it up — communication! I believe we are in the embryonic stage of this phenomenon, but so much of this is beginning to happen that we need to consider it! Who knows, maybe thoughts will replace e-mails and cell phones. If so, there will be no need for a network of towers to relay our messages.

Is there a spiritual explanation? I feel a little like what Edgar Cayce, the "sleeping prophet," must have felt when he went to sleep and retrieved in dreams information requested. While I was "half asleep" this seemingly clear thought came to me — the Christ-in-me communicated, or spoke, to the Christ-in-them. Anyhow, the very thing I spoke about three days earlier, about calling on the phone, took place — right before our very eyes. No effort. Just thinking!

If this be true — and I must confess that it is new to me — can even this be a form of God speaking? The God-in-me talking to the God-in-them!

Such a conclusion is becoming less farfetched to me as I am moving forward in my spirit-journey.

What say you?

CHAPTER I

"*I told you NO!*"

And, am I glad He did! I heard God, in a voice deep within my being, speak in a loud voice, clearly unmistakably... *"I TOLD YOU NO — DON'T YOU EVEN OPEN YOUR MOUTH!"*

This is to encourage all of you who have been discouraged at "NO" answers. Allow me to put this in perspective.

The place was in Kentucky, the time was 1986. The exact location was on Interstate 64 — just outside Lexington.

Edna and I were living near Charleston, W.Va. I had been out of a church as pastor for a year. That was back when I still thought "ministry" was inside a specially-designed building with pews, pulpits and all that "stuff!"

T.T. May had been my dear trusted friend for 34 years. Tom was pastor of a non-denominational community church in Lexington and he wanted to retire. But there was a problem: who do you get to follow you? Tom was trying to choose me, which was an honor, and I was trying to choose him — that is to become Tom's associate and then pastor.

It was a good, even GREAT idea! It offered about everything I had dreamed of. Association with long-time friends within a university city. I could see a far reaching T.V. ministry! I could envision being near two of my alma maters — Asbury Seminary and Southern Seminary in Louisville. By now I had my doctorate, I was *somebody* and surely these colleagues would recognize that and accept me. Oh, it was a great idea. I wanted to accept Tom's gracious offer and get back into the flow of things! Especially after Tom said to me, "God told me you are the man!" I was excited! I couldn't wait!

Well, God had not "told" me! And even though it appeared to be the right thing to do I was struggling with accepting his offer. Tom saw that and suggested, "Oscar, why don't you take six weeks — come over here on the weekends and see if you get the feel for it. Then decide. You can do whatever you want ... preach, pray, sing, play the piano."

So, for the next six weeks we did just that! Some weekends I would be high on the idea — the next my spirit would sort of drag. Somehow in the pit of my stomach, it did not feel right. Sometimes there would be a tightness in my lower stomach. My spirit was trying to tell me something, "This is not right!"

At the close of the six weeks — on Easter Sunday, 1986 — I had to give Tom an answer. I'll never forget the emotional moment when I told him, "Tom, I am honored that you have considered me to be associated with you in this church!" With tears in my eyes, I said, "Tom, we can't accept it." He replied, "Oscar, I knew you were going to say that."

A relief came over me and we drove off — back to a little trailer park we had purchased in West Virginia, some four hours away.

Monday came. I had one of those famous "Monday morning quarterback" sessions with Edna. I said to her, "Who are we to be turning down an offer from anybody? We don't have anything (speaking of an active, ministerial career) and I am saying 'no?' We could accept the offer temporarily and then when something else comes along we could accept that. This thing is so crucial (besides that we were going broke financially), that it's worth another 24 hours. Why don't I call Tom and go back one more time — today — just to see if we missed it!" She agreed. So I called Tom and headed back to Lexington.

Just before reaching the city, I heard a voice, *"I TOLD YOU NO — DON'T YOU EVEN OPEN YOUR MOUTH!"* Clear, distinct, loud (all within my being — no "outside" voices!) Who was it? It was God! At least we were on speaking terms and I took comfort in that!

I arrived at Tom's house and after a few moments of general conversation, we went out to eat — would you believe, at a BAR-B-Q restaurant?

I hope you see the irony of this as our final life's dream was not far away as we were "led" into one of the most successful restaurant ventures in the nation — what is today "Col. Poole's Georgia BAR-B-Q, Inc.!"

We visited and spent the night with Tom and Bertha — then left the next morning and never said a word about the subject of going to work with Tom in the church! That's been 18 years ago, and I have often wondered what Tom thought about that brief return trip! I always wondered. Maybe he thought I was crazy, or whatever. It had to seem strange. Tom has since passed away and I may never know what he thought!

CHAPTER II

"I want you to return to Georgia!"

I have left Tom's house and I am headed home to Charleston with Edna waiting for me. I had not even discussed the matter with Tom — case closed!

I am "bouncing" along Highway 64 near Winchester, Ky., in our nearly worn-out white Chevette. My spirit is settled. I am relaxed because I had obeyed God!

When all of a sudden — out of the blue — that voice returned! This time it was not loud — but that "still, small voice" you read about in 1 Kings 19! It was casual. It was conversational. The voice spoke. Then I spoke. Now, here's a man "hearing a voice" and no one is in the car with him! It is God Himself! Who else?

He said to me, *"Where, after all these years, did I bless you the most?"*

I thought for a moment. "In the mountains of north Georgia!" I said.

"*Where were you the happiest and most content?*"

I replied, "In the mountains of north Georgia!"

"*Where did you prosper the most in all the years of your ministry?*"

I said, "In the mountains of north Georgia!"

"*Where did your family call 'home'?*"

"In the mountains of north Georgia!"

This was almost getting boring, repetitive, redundant — "In the mountains of north Georgia!" But I see now that He (God) was pulling it out of me and causing me to say the very answer to the culmination of my life's pursuit — the mountains of north Georgia!"

Then came that loud voice again, the one I had heard the day before — almost in the same place on the same highway — "*I WANT YOU TO RETURN TO THE MOUNTAINS OF NORTH GEORGIA!*"

Wow! I had heard from God. I almost shouted! Relief! I had found the answer to my quest — I had HEARD from God! He had, in the very midst of my confusion, spoken.

I could not wait to get back with Edna to tell her the good news!

I arrived at our trailer home in West Virginia. I sat Edna down.

"Edna," I said, almost embarrassingly, but with

great joy and relief. "Guess where we are going?"

She stared and waited.

"BACK TO THE MOUNTAINS OF NORTH GEORGIA!"

Within three months we moved to "the mountains of north Georgia!' But even when we got there it took some "doings" to finally arrive at the destination which became world-renowned — the BAR-B-Q forum — notice I said "forum" — a newer and *very* different pulpit for ministry!

CHAPTER III

∽

"If I don't come back on that date, you must seek Me for a whole new view of Eschatology!"

The scene shifts to the town of Ocala in central Florida, where I was going to try "one more time" an "Oscar thing" — build a GREAT CHURCH ... for God! We still maintained an established connection in (you guessed it!) the mountains of north Georgia!

I, along with Edna, who has faithfully stood by me for over 54 years, were going — I repeat, "one last time," to build this great church! After all, I was born and reared in Florida, raised in a tourist environment, knew the people — and all that kind of rationale. This, as you will shortly see, was not to be, and it was the last time!

While there for about a year, God spoke again! It

seems that God has spoken to me when I have been about doing "wrong things"! This time the wrong thing was attempting to build a home for God!

It was the summer of 1988. Word got out that Jesus was coming back during the Jewish feast of Rosh Hashanah, Sept. 13, 14, 15. A man named Whisnant had written a book, *"Eighty-eight reasons Christ Will Return in '88."* Although I really did not believe it, I wasn't sure. I was discouraged — even depressed — and I hoped He would! Emotionally I was ready "to get out of this mess" called "the world!" I WANTED OUT!

Allow me to say that of all the writings on the subject of the "second coming" of Christ, that is with all the attendant talk of a rapture, tribulation, 70 weeks, new temple to be built in Jerusalem, etc., I think Whisnant did a thorough and most complete job of articulating this point of view. Certainly, he must be right (except for the date-setting — we all know better than to do that!). After all, this view of the eschaton (end-times) must be right since the majority of Bible-believing Christians believed this scenario to be true, including the famed Billy Graham, Hal Lindsey, Jerry Falwell, the Pentecostals, the Baptists, old line Methodists — all of which I admired and respected. And, although I did not know what I really believed, I hoped Whisnant was right.

So I made myself ready! I volunteered to preach at the maximum security prison at Cross City, Fla. I had read Matthew 25 and just in case Jesus was coming I wanted to be ready!

Rosh Hashanah came, September 13, 14, and 15. I sat there awaiting the "shout!"

He didn't come!

Was I disappointed! As I said earlier, I didn't think he would, but a little hope had risen within me. During the closing day of the given time frame, the author of the book told the world he had missed it by one day — so I waited one more day! Well, He has not come yet, and if He did, we've been "left behind!"

It was during this time that I heard the voice inside me which I very discernably knew was the God that had spoken before. It said, *"If I don't come back during this time, you must seek Me for a whole new view of eschatology!"*

God threw me a curve

I saw a picture of myself standing at home plate. God was the pitcher and He threw me a curve! That's how I interpreted this whole scenario!

To make a long story short it began to be impressed upon my mind and spirit that I should — once and for all — give up on the "big church" idea, return to the mountains of north Georgia, find a place for the 8' x 12' BAR-B-

Q trailer that was sitting on Tom and Naomi's farm, and go to work selling BAR-B-Q. It was the only thing that made sense. So we returned, found a place for the one-room carry-out trailer, and went to work selling BAR-B-Q. But before I tell you how we found the place, let me say a few words about how my "whole new view of eschatology" came about.

So I am moving ahead a little as God works through space, time, matter and motion (Einstein) as mentioned in my earlier book, *Speak-To-It*. Then I will return in the next chapter and relate to you how that it was God "speaking to me" that led us to the place I have just mentioned.

Through a strange set of circumstances I was led to examine the "preterist" view of eschatology — that all this noise about Jesus returning literally through the skies, a rapture, a subsequent tribulation and on and on myth, and that most of the "end times" talk in the Bible was already realized or occurred between 67 and 70 AD. In other words, what the majority of Christians are looking for to take place in the near future was already fulfilled (past tense) and has already happened!

I had run across this preterist view over 40 years earlier while in seminary, but paid little attention to it because I had no interest in end-times. It seems like I've always been more concerned about the here and now, now more than ever!

Let me divert from the text to mention that Edna and I are parked in the Wal-Mart parking lot at Princeton, W.Va., three hours removed from Doughton Park on the Blue Ridge Parkway back in N.C. You can see that we are "moving on" in this little journey. I believe a tidbit of this information allows the reader to actually become a "part" of the writing of this book. Truly besides the traveling — the writing itself is an adventure!

Another sideline thought. I was just sharing with Edna how excited and free my spirit seems to be as I am reliving these truths that I have learned and experienced since much of what I am sharing in this book has taken place! It seems that even as I am sharing, what I have experienced as truth is setting me free all over again!

The downside to all this is ... do I have any friends left? I hope I do not have to trade friends for the truth — but if so, as painful as that might be — I have chosen the latter! There's nothing — absolutely nothing — like being free in your spirit! I am having a wonderful time in the writing of this book!

Let's get back on track! Oh yes, the preterist view of eschatology!

Without going into some treatise on the subject, let me recommend John L. Bray's book, *Matthew 24 Fulfilled* that I mentioned in the book, *Speak-To-It*. I have spoken with John Bray several times on the phone. He is a retired 82-year-old Southern Baptist missionary-evangelist-statesman, who lives in Lakeland, Fla., and is a member of the First Baptist Church of that city. You can receive a copy of his book, the finest I have ever seen on the subject, by writing to him at: John L. Bray, P.O. Box 90129, Lakeland, FL 33804.

John will not sell you the book but he will give it to you! He remains stubborn about this and will make no exceptions as I have tried to purchase at least 30 copies to loan out.

I don't have the time or energy, nor interest, to go into the matter extensively, so if you are interested you will have to make your own search as I did. If you ever come to see me at our home in Georgia or elsewhere, I'll be glad to sit down and share with you as time allows, but other than that I believe too much time on the end and not enough time on the now can become a waste of time!

Having said the above, I will mention just a few of my views on the subject here. I believe much of the problem of last days theology has to do with a literal interpretation of scripture versus an allegorical or metaphorical interpretation. Remember that most of Jesus' teachings were just this, He spoke to them in parables.

As far as the timing goes, I believe all of what Jesus said in Matthew 24 was fulfilled in that generation! Those "standing there!" This includes Daniel 12 and the Book of Revelation! All of this was "realized" between 67 & 70 A.D., with the destruction of Jerusalem! I think the stars falling and the elements burned up are metaphorical and were metaphors known to the Jewish people of that day — not ours. The "abomination of desolation" happened centuries ago. There will be no temple rebuilt — there is no need for such! God is not a "backing up" God, nor in retreat — He is always forward!

In Matthew 24 the word "world" referred to was "age." One age was ending and a new one beginning. Those were the "last days" spoken by the prophets including the writer of Hebrews when he spoke of "these last days!" He was referring (literally) to the days he was living in — not ours!

I think most of the present "last days" theologians, especially those screaming on T.V., are "pundits" and don't know what they are talking about! You can send your money to them if you want to, but count me out! I have no interest in building up their million dollar homes. "Think," I said. "Think about it!"

Again, I say this is not a treatise on eschatology, but I thought I ought to give a little follow-up to what I heard God say to me.

A Sign Following

God is no "strange" God, but He often acts or behaves in strange ways! I am going to share one with you. You Pentecostal folks will be at home with this. A "sign following" is defined as something happening after an event to confirm or affirm that what has happened is authentic or true. Now, when God speaks I don't think you have to have a sign following, but I do feel this happens. One such time is the following...

I was only one or two pages from writing this chapter on eschatology, when I found myself in a laundromat in Sparta, N.C., waiting for Edna to finish our laundry. I had been asleep on a comfortable chair in the back of the store. (Notice the picture — Edna working and me sleeping! I knew you would, I just thought I'd admit it.)

Half asleep, I looked up and there was a young lady, Sharon Clark, asking the manager for change. I asked, "You from around here?"

"Yes," she replied.

"What do you do?" I asked. (Those of you who know me can picture this!)

"Oh, I produce videos for children and I write books," she said.

"That's what I do!" I said. "In fact, I'm writing one right now and just took a break to come with my wife to town to wash clothes!"

Then I said, "What church do you attend?" (I often ask this as it gives me some idea as to what spectrum a person lives in — not that it's any of my business!)

She hesitated, the air between us got a little dense

(metaphor for awkward).

"Well," she said, "I guess it might be like Baptist." Then she added, "Ever hear of covenant realized eschatology?"

"You mean preterist?" I replied.

You should have seen the aghast look on her face! She almost fell in the floor — not physically but metaphorically. She could not believe this. Nor hardly could I!

Here I was one or two pages away from writing this "eschatological" material (this big word inserted to let some of you know I've been to school). I am half-asleep, minding my own business. Up walks this attractive young lady. Asks for change. We get into a conversation and before you know it — about an hour later — she leads me to meet John Anderson and his lovely wife, Ann Marie, at their world headquarters just down the street. I knew nothing of these people. I did not know that I was two city blocks away from mutual friends of John Bray, and that John speaks live to approximately two and one half million listeners around the world several times per week!

"What's going on here?" I am asking and wondering. Just three days earlier the "thinking" about Ralph and Gerri — now this?!

We spent an exciting hour together. You should have been there. Ann Marie is about the best ventriloquist

I've ever heard. She has traveled extensively all over the world giving programs to huge audiences. She once worked with E. J. Daniels and with Claude Bowers, now the owner-CEO of T.V. Channel 55 in Orlando, Florida.

Here Edna and I are at the most prestigious center for the whole preterist movement and what a discussion we are having! I gave them a copy of my book, *Speak-To-It*. They filled a box with their materials, videos, books by other authors on the preterist subject, including several little books by John L. Bray — my friend and theirs! I do not know where this "coming together" will lead, but I am thrilled and excited just thinking about it!

Every year in May they host a conference on eschatology in Sparta. I have a strong idea we'll be there! If you want to know about these folks you may look them up on their website, www. lighthouseworldministries.com, or www.lighthouseproductionsllc.com, or your may call them at 336-372-9600. Or you may go to a laundromat in Sparta!

Maybe you're thinking what I am thinking ... this may be a sign following, confirming my preterist view. I really don't know, and don't need to know. It's just another one of those strange or bizarre events.

Authors Note: We are still here at the Wal-Mart parking lot in our motorhome in Princeton, W.Va. I have just returned from visiting with the world headquarters of the Wisdom Channel, located just nine miles down the road in Bluefield. I have desired, even felt led, to make this contact for three or four years. I met the director and left some materials. I have felt spiritually connected with them for several years, especially with Carolyn Craft, who was formerly associated with them. I got her phone number and plan to call her shortly. I wonder what will become of this? Doesn't matter, except that I obeyed the still small voice within!

CHAPTER IV

"If you get on the side of that hill and do the menial work, I'll show the world what I will do!"

That inner strange voice again!

I few pages back I mentioned about looking for a place to set up our 8' x 12' BAR-B-Q business.

Edna and I looked over the area. We were living in the Blue Ridge area near Mineral Bluff. Somehow we felt an inner urge to look for a place 15 miles away in Ellijay, Ga., where our successful church ministry took place years earlier. While scanning for possible sights we noticed that trucks were digging out the mountain in the heart of East Ellijay on Highway 515 — the "Zell Miller Parkway" — the main four-lane thoroughfare built in recent years.

We were drawn to it. Began to ask questions. No one had any plans for it. They were moving the dirt off the mountain and dumping it into a hole across the street between the service road and the main highway.

What were they really doing? Preparing the new location for what has now become a north Georgia landmark and legend! The dirt placed in the ditch across the street became a paved parking lot (40 cars) for a "Park & Ride" area for the public to park their cars and carpool to and from their jobs toward Atlanta. But it was empty on weekends — that is, until Poole's BAR-B-Q began to explode and the lot filled up with customers! A quarter-million dollar parking lot — not even for the asking.

Well, we rented the side of the hill for $100 per month. Borrowed more money and went to work selling BAR-B-Q! The first days receipts were $208, and half of that was profit.

The real story that unfolded since is that of a rags-to-riches story, sort of a Cinderella one! Sometimes as I look back, I'm not even sure it's real.

I plan to write a more detailed history of our legend later this fall and winter while we are traveling in Florida and Arizona, but I must tell what God said in reference to this location of the road-side shack, and a few perspectives and events that have followed! Hang on! It's hard to believe!

The Voice

While considering the hillside, fast being emptied of dirt, *God spoke again!* Just as the title of this chapter states — and precisely in these exact words, *"If you get on the side of that hill and do the menial work, I'll show the world what I will do!"*

Am I glad that my spiritual growth and new understandings of how God works was operative and, am I glad that not only did I believe that *God speaks today,* but am I glad I *heard* Him!

And, the "menial" work we did! Edna and I worked 12 hours a day, 7 days per week. The two of us spent 168 man hours per week! We did the work of four! We sold BAR-B-Q! Two and three hundred dollars worth per day! This was big for us!

They laughed! The place was tacky, so tacky it was "classic." We added a room — a 10' x 10' porch where we could watch T.V. between customers. The business grew to three and four hundred dollars per day, and we hired a part-time helper. Edna and I were able to "take off" a half day now and then. One day a customer arrived and found our helper asleep on the porch while he was watching T.V. She had to wake him up! "Sir, could you serve me some BAR-B-Q?!"

Here is a funny one! We decided we should sell french fries. So, we got a fry daddy, big enough to fry one small order at a time. It was right out on the front where everyone could see it! Three men were in line awaiting their orders. I'll never forget — Ermel Forrester — as he waited — his french fries cooking! He told me later that he said to another man in line, "I like that old boy! He has pretty good BAR-B-Q, but he'll never make it!"

Every time I see him I remind him of what he said!

Oh — the room we added had a roof from off a chicken house. Literally. We placed two card tables in it for inside seating. We put plastic around the sides to keep the rain out.

It was "tacky." We built a small storage room outside for supplies — even put a toilet and a sink in it.

Then we added another room, this one with materials Fred Bailey gave me from tearing down a room he had added to a mobile home on his property. As a lasting memorial you can still see the name "Fred Bailey" on a plaque on the front door!

I must mention about the birth of the pigs scattered around which became the "seen around the world" PIG-HILL-OF-FAME!

The day before we opened I noticed we needed a new "Open-Close" sign. I thought, "I'll go down to the feed store. They'll have a picture of a pig on a feed sack. I'll copy it and make a cute little sign." So I went to Carl Hill's local feed store and wound up with a pig-image (the Oscar Poole version) and solved the problem!

But now I had a new problem — I had some plywood left over! So I made about six more and stuck them around with mine and Edna's, plus Mark, Carl, Fred, Bob and Melissa's names on them. This was done very timidly as I thought they might hit me! But they didn't and soon others asked for their pig — then others — and this is how the world-famous PIG-HILL-OF-FAME was born! Just that innocently and simply.

Before long there were 137 pigs on the hill!

Two Associated Press reporters stopped by to eat. They enquired about the pigs on the hill. I told them what I told you above. I noticed the lady was making notes as I spoke. "We're from the Associated Press," she said. "And we sense a story here!" That was Thursday, and by Sunday we were in over 1,000 newspapers world-wide — a picture of me in the midst of the pigs!

And, the business DOUBLED in ONE DAY — that day from about $500 to $1,000! "Help, HELP!"

From there it has grown to ten times that amount and still growing!

While several were laughing at our silliness and tackiness, a traveler from the Swedish Embassy in Washington D.C. stopped by. He was taken by our place. "This place is so tacky, it's classic!" he said. "This is the most Americana place I've seen throughout my travels."

I asked him if he would write this to the local Chamber of Commerce, which he did, and that has become a prized document and is on permanent display in our restaurant! The man was the "cultural counselor" for the Washington, D.C. Swedish Embassy.

So now we are "cultured" — a new kind, with "folk art" and all! There became a little less laughing. The "so tacky it's classic" has become one of our legendary trademarks. It has stuck!

I saw we had something here. Who wouldn't? This was folk art and I was the artist!

Moby heard about the pigs and sent word that he wanted one. (Moby is the number one country-western disc jockey in America, and at the time, 1992, was associated with Kicks 101.5 in Atlanta.) For the next three months that's all he talked about — his pig on Poole's Hill! So, we made him the "Chief Pig" — a large pig on top of the hill. He remains there today.

Pat Buchanan for President

Then Pat came! In February of 1992 he began his entire southern crusade at our BAR-B-Q with national and international coverage! I was standing with Pat and Shelly at the front door as they walked out, a reporter snapped a picture of me with them holding their pig — it was on the front page of the San Francisco Chronicle the next day as well as hundreds of others! Five hundred people gathered in one day at our "tacky" place.

Media from all over the world — literally — covered the event. CNN, ABC, NBC, CBS, AP, CBC, Reuters, newspapers, magazines — even M-TV (I would not have believed this one unless I had seen it with my own eyes, sitting in our PIG-MOBY-IL!).

By now you are asking, "What's going on here? Is all this true? Is it for real?" If you are asking this, what do you think was going on within me? (I'll tell you more about this in my sequel book which follows in a few months! It will give, in more detail, the whole story of Col. Poole's Georgia BAR-B-Q.)

I am giving you just a little of our story — especially in the early stages — to show you that while Edna and I were continuing with the "menial" work, God was "showing the world what He would do," as He had SAID! Remember, this is a book primarily on when God spoke to me, but I am including not only God *speaking*, but God *doing*!

One day a reporter stopped by and asked, "How does one get on the hill?" I responded immediately in the *THEN* moment, spontaneously — having never even thought about it before — "You must qualify in three ways: You must have an honest face, good intentions, and $3.00!" (It has since gone to $5.00.)

This is still the answer people receive when they ask the question!

The BAR-B-Q continues today — growing — ever

expanding (even as Edna and I are in our motorhome in Beckley, W.Va.! These pages are being written here!)

The restaurant now seats 180 inside with 30 or 40 on the "snoutside!" There is a new paved parking lot surrounding the edifice with the hill moved back to accommodate more pigs! In fact, we took 4,000 little pigs (they are now made of plastic to last longer) and made them into one giant pig shape, perhaps the size of 40 or 50 billboards! This, I think, has become our "signature-pig!"

Col. Poole's Georgia BAR-B-Q has become a landmark and legend in "the mountains of north Georgia!" Remember that phrase in Chapter 2?

The eatery is home to the TAJ-MA-HOG, the HOG ROCK CAFE, and the world-famous PIG-HILL-OF-FAME! Sales have soared into the millions and we are still expanding!

CHAPTER V

"A Rhema Word"

This chapter deals with what some of you know as a *"rhema"* word. That is, sometimes He speaks through a written word (the *"Logos* Word"). Sometimes one may read a verse from the Bible and the spirit within *enlivens* it — makes it come alive! But even this *making it alive* is a form of a direct communication.

In this case the Bible verse is Rev. 12:11. Here's what I heard within myself. *"They* (that's us) *overcame him* (that's the adversary — my views about a devil and evil have changed — but there are adversaries or obstacles to overcome) *by the blood of the Lamb* (that's the price that God paid for all this) *and by the WORD* (spoken or released) *of our TESTIMONY* (truths we have experienced or lived out!)" This is not theoretical or oratorical sermons, but practical theology. I call it theology that hits the road! (Our road being Highway 515!)

Testimony

As I have indicated earlier, I believe testimonies have taken the place of preaching — simply sharing what God has said and done *within* and *through* you!

As Rev. 12:11 was *coming alive* within me, I heard God's voice directly, *"I am building a testimony through you ... when it is finished you can tell others* (testify)."

I began to see that this was even how the Bible was written! That they did it — then wrote about it! They didn't even have a theology for writing the Bible! Except a few had scrolls of the Old Testament (very few — the original 12 disciples didn't, I think it is safe to say).

They were *led from within* themselves — by the Holy Spirit who had come to in-dwell them! Just like it is with you and me.

I referred to this in the earlier book, *Speak-To-It!* when I told a dead group of orthodox Christians in New York once, that "for what we (Travis Tatum and I) were doing, the theology had not been written!" I was embarrassed but I have discovered that this is true.

Robert Schuller, I had noticed, had proved this by his experiences. He lived it and then wrote about it. This has become an indelibly impressed insight that developed within me as I lived out and moved forward as I was spoken to and led from within myself.

So, to make a longer story shorter, we are now

telling and writing about all these matters — a *testimony*!

Well, it's simple — there was nothing to tell about in 1992 regarding the events that have happened since, but only conjecture! Now, after 12 years, we have something to tell about. We have experienced — *lived* — everything I am telling you.

I mention again Einstein, regarding the "12 years" mentioned above. God, the eternal constant, works through space-time-matter-motion, at least as far as this earth plane is concerned. It takes time — quality time.

This makes God relevant (related) to all that is. Another way of saying it — the spirit works through space, time and matter.

If it's new, it's now!

You see, if it's *new*, it's *now*! And if it's *now* it's *new* — and it's never been done before! No past models. No past theology. No rule book! It's *new* — it's *now*.

It's a new day! The scriptures declare, "Behold, I make *all things new*" (Rev. 21:5).

Dear reader — I hope you are still my friend — open your eyes to the frontier that is before us! It's *right here* — and *now*! You and I are privileged to be involved in this *greatest of all dramas*! We, with God and each other, can save our world — and make things happen — for we are persons with great ability. Knowing who we are, whose we are, and where we are going — we (you and I) *can do all things through Christ which strengtheneth us* — from the Christ within!

Most of what I am doing now is *testifying* — simply telling the story of how I heard from God within myself and then set out to do what He said.

You could call this "responsibility" — in this case our *response* to His *ability*. It is He (God), not us, yet it is us — God working out of the Spirit (timeless constant). It is He and us in a harmonious, creative relationship!

In other words it is God's Word (what He told me directly) put in motion (Einstein again!). No chapter, no verse (except the *rhema* example given above), no well-known Bible prophet — just God and me!

I remind you that's what this book is about: God speaking now! Within the context of our natural lives! I say natural for the benefit of Glen Bowen, with whom I maintain an active dialogue — sometimes agreeing and often not. I've been trying to say there is no difference between the natural or the spiritual! It's all one! Nature and spirit are connected together. (See my book, *Speak-To-It*, defining matter as "spirit slowed down to visibility!")

I have another friend who is still trapped into first century, third party God-talking scenarios, whom I would love to see delivered from the mental illusion that God quit talking in 95 A.D. But that is not really my business — I'm simply "testifying!"

CHAPTER VI

∽

"You must seek Me for a whole new view of everything!"

What?! You think I struck out down there in Florida in 1988 — when I returned to the north Georgia Mountains. I lost the whole world series! (Metaphor — not literal — as I can't even throw a baseball! If some of you fundamentalists can understand me talking metaphorically — why can't you do the same with bible writers when they speak in metaphors?

We had just gotten started in our little BAR-B-Q business. I had just put the day's meat supply on the pit when — you guessed it! — that voice spoke again! (Now, as you will see, I'm not liking what I am hearing! In fact, I am threatened by it!)

Between the pit and the 8' x 12' shack, I heard God say, *"Not only must you seek Me for a whole new view of escha-*

tology, but you must seek Me for a whole new view of everything!"

Just who is God talking to? Doesn't he know that I spent ten professional years in college, university and theological seminary? That I had earned two bachelors and two masters and one doctorate — having sat at the feet of some of the most recognized scholars of our day? That I had received one of the highest degrees (accredited by the folks that know God-things) in theology (the study of God-matters). That I had studied Greek and Hebrew? That I had been chosen "Minister-of-the-Year" three times and my ministry had been selected as one of one hundred most creative ministries within my denomination? (United Methodist, Tidings, 1971.)

I was nearly insulted! I had been there and done that! I was one of the boys!

What am I to do? Throw it all away? Well, in the subsequent ten years that followed, I remained a prophet in exile in the north Georgia Mountains, building a world-class BAR-B-Q, listening and thinking about a whole new journey of faith!

Yes, ten years in exile. No one to teach me! Very few books, oh, one now and then. Mostly just God and me.

A great change came upon and within me! Not all at once, but sort of like a metamorphosis, little by little.

A New Perspective of Optimism

For one thing, my perspective changed. I changed from a pessimist to an optimist! I began to see things differently, *much* differently! I changed my image from one working *for* God to one working *with* God! I spent much time in the *secret place*.

I found myself in the woods, forest glens. I went to the mountains, the oceans and seas. I liked this new house of God! It had no pulpits, hard pews (it did have some hard rocks!), none of that "old stuff." But it did have purple mountain grandeur, lily pads, blue skies. Whippoorwills — and trees that sang! I felt at home there. I *belonged* there. I heard God speak in whispers as the wind blew softly through the trees. I heard Him in the storms as the lightning flashed and the thunders rolled! I began to enjoy my new surroundings and hardly ever wanted to leave! There was *inspiration* there! You could, and I did, *hear* God there!

So, I return there often! Further, I am not alone when I go there! I am surrounded by music, the presence of God there sets my heart to singing! I hear orchestras, symphonies, hymns. I am blessed!

A New Appreciation for Nature

I guess I am slipping into changes that have

occurred in me during this new transition in my life. I am gaining an appreciation that had not been there before — and I've begun to actively participate in it. Others have experienced this as I — here's where the great retreat centers are located: Junaluska, Montreat, Ridgecrest (I see I'm getting carried away!) — and God has placed me in a great place where I can hear Him — in the mountains of north Georgia!

I am, right now, as I am writing this little book, winding my way through a great spiritual corridor — up from our little town of East Ellijay, Ga., — through Junaluska, Asheville, Winston-Salem, the Blue Ridge Parkway through Doughton Park, Sparta, Wythville, Va., Bluefield, Beckley — on to Charleston (Edna's home), then finally over into the Ohio Amish country, where I hope to finish this writing. The inspiration for sharing this testimony has simply flowed. I have written faster than I can write and I hope Keli can read it!

What am I saying? That I have a new appreciation for nature! God seems to be here in a big way. He speaks here! You can *hear* Him here! My new theology (new understandings of truth) have certainly helped in this — that matter is spirit slowed down to visibility!

A New Peace

I remind the reader that I heard "...*seek Me for new*

views of everything!" Well, it has been over ten years now and I will try to describe some of these new views! All of this has come about as a result of walking and talking with deity (God) — and He speaking to me. I have heard Him in the deepest night, in the morning and twilight, at noon, and the evening sunsets. A newer, more serene peace has overtaken me as I am witnessing a new heaven and a new earth — right before my eyes — and I am a partaker in it!

A New Self-Image

A new self-image has emerged. I am the very offspring of God! I can do what He does. And so can you! And you! We're *somebody*! We're not average! We can experience greatness because we are part of Someone great — God! We are in active communication with Him. *"This is my Father's world — I rest me in the thought that though the wrong seems oft so strong — God is still the ruler yet!"* He speaks to me everywhere!

The hymn *"In the Garden"* has come alive! *"I come to the garden alone, while the dew is still on the roses. And the voice I hear falling on my ear, the son of God discloses! And He walks with me and He talks with me, and He tells me I am His own! And the joy we share as we tarry there — none other has ever known!"*

All this and more — it's a right now thing! *"Heaven*

has come down and glory has filled my soul!" It seems when I hear these words that a great symphony fills the air! You ought to hear the surround sound! It's all around us — everywhere! Listen, and all this worshipful singing has not been just on Sundays! It's been every day — except when I have focused on other matters.

The Eternal Now

I have discovered that eternity is now. We're in it! Not will be, but now! These are therefore divine moments! Oh, the joy of His presence (notice that even this word is "present!") Simple? Probably not; somehow I had missed it with all that professionalism about God, the Bible, being a Christian, etc. Time has a new meaning! Today is now! And when I get to tomorrow it will be another now, and so on! This is exciting — nearly every sentence has an exclamation mark!

How the Universe Works

I have a new understanding of how the uni-verse (one verse) works! In the midst of this symphony (together sounds) I have discovered that "basic matter seems to have the capacity to respond to a loving person!" and I have proven it. From my experience during this new period in my life, it appears that I have had the privilege of "directing" some of these neutrons, electrons and molecules into newer forms (little pigs on a hill, oh how silly, yet classical). New situations, and I have created some of it!

Hear God Through Others?

Maybe I have learned to hear (or at least discern) the voice of God through other people. Such "trite" terms as TAJ-MA-HOG, HOG ROCK CAFE, and the PIG-HILL-OF-FAME all came to me as I listened to what others had to say. Were they inspired? Or what? Does God bother with mundane matters?

Even as I am suggesting that I have heard God through others (as I write this in Beckley, W.Va. it seems I am hearing affirmation from within me — sort of like, "*Yes, Amen and Amen...*") — like a witness on the inside? Oh well, this is exciting ... even fun!

I remember one day while some friends were laughing at my silliness, that I said, "I want to do for the pig what Walter did for the mouse!" I could sort of imagine that Mr. and Mrs. Disney's son came home one day from school and exclaimed, "I want to name my pet mouse Mickey! And how about Donald for that little duck out in the yard? Maybe Pluto for our dog?" I thought, "Is what we are doing any sillier than what Walt Disney did?"

Also, one day, it was my privilege to address the local Chamber of Commerce, the one that the Swedish Embassy Cultural Counselor wrote to about our "tacky place." I said to them, "I may be silly — but the sillier I get the more money I make!" They laughed — not at me, but with me!

Well, whatever. Silly or not silly, here we are located on Georgia Highway 515 — where the whole world seems to be driving by, with many stopping in to see their pigs and eat! Seriously, I think there is a theology for this. It's called JOY — one of the fruit of the spirit! Is God ever silly? Since all of this is an expression of His, I think so. I think He even laughs out loud! Seems as though I've heard Him!

Imagery and Words

I have learned that God works through imagery (images, visions) and words, especially when spoken or released. All those pigs on the hill formed sort of a public psyche (mental image). People saw it — their own names. They got the overall picture and this image remained with them. They talked it — the power of spoken words. They did all over the world — in Shang Hai, Indonesia, London, Vienna, Africa, Italy, New York — I'm not kidding — actual reports have come to us! The above cities saw us on T.V. and T-shirts. Our mayor himself saw someone wearing a Col. Poole's Georgia BAR-B-Q T-shirt in London!

The Yellow Suit

That, too is imagery. I was attending the Republican National Convention in San Diego in 1996. I sat behind a delegate with a "strange" hat! The media interviewed him and made all over him!

"You wait," I said to myself, "until I get home!"

This gave birth to my yellow suit with an Uncle Sam top hat! I wear it to rallies and conventions. I was even on the front page of the *Los Angeles Times!* Also on CNN and other media. Now Edna has a suit just like it — we wore them to the recent Georgia State G.O.P. Convention in Columbus, Ga., and I made the front page even there! Edna and I both plan to attend the upcoming National Convention at Madison Square Garden in New York City three weeks from now! (New York City?!!)

During these following years of the late eighties and early nineties of hearing God speak, it has been revealed to me the profound meaning of this word — imagery!

Even God Himself uses and works through imaginations! He sees a thing before He does it! So do we as His offspring! You see, we have His very nature. We too, have visions and do not perish, but prosper. Of course, this imagination business is not new, but I have come to appreciate, understand, and to actually experience it in greater depths — simply by wearing a yellow suit!

U.S. Capitol, Washington D.C.

A word about the yellow suit and Washington — D.C. that is!

We have been blessed and privileged to take our BAR-B-Q to our nation's capitol for eight years in a row. Once we parked the PIG-MOBY-IL on the Capitol steps for one full day! There is a pig-ture of it on the back cover of *Speak-To-It*, the earlier book. In and out of office buildings, the rotundas, up and down steps — many on Capitol Hill know me from the yellow suit. I've had my pig-ture taken with groups from all over the U.S. and the world. I've done this so much that I almost forget about it!

Yes, there is a deep and profound theological meaning to imagery, and I am still learning about it! Proud? Yes, in a way! But deep within me there is a true humility as I associate God with wearing the suit! Joe McCutchen calls this my "million dollar" suit!

I share this imagery theme as a part of my re-orientation to life as I have followed the pursuits of hearing from God!

The Old and the New

When God spoke a *"whole new view of everything,"* of course, my spirit knew that it was a figure of speech — not literally everything, but this time, instead of a metaphor, it was a hyperbole! You mean God exaggerates? Well, one of the N.T. writers did when he wrote that he "supposed the whole world could not contain all the books" if what Jesus said and did were written! Remember the figures of speech we learned in junior high school? This is one of the points I am trying to make — that like us, God speaks in metaphors, allegories, even, as in my case, hyperbole.

So what we have here is a convergence with old and the new! But I guess that's probably the way it should be, when one gets my age things should become synergized — come together! The term "God is great" never changes — except maybe to say "He is GREATER" as our awareness expands. I suppose one way to say it is that while some things never change, our awareness or perceptions do. We begin to see old things in new ways! But we must add that there are new things never seen before!

Realized Eschatology

I have already alluded to this change in me! I saw this a little over ten years ago — that what most people are looking to happen already happened between 67 and 70 A.D. I'll not repeat myself here except to say it is a big relief when one comes to the place that he no longer worries about the world being blown up — although I admit freely that I am deeply concerned about world terrorism, as I know that you are! That must be stopped and sometimes our choices appear to be the lesser of two evils!

I think the biggest blessing from the change in me is I can "get on" with the rest of life in helping to establish a spiritual kingdom of peace on earth, good will to men!

I was in a home where a friend was reading — can you believe it? A novel on being "left behind!" Following a cataclysmic interruption by God in history, a to-be-dreaded coming event — somehow the schizophrenic idea of getting happy about the destruction of the world is worked into the "last days" scenario! I noticed the book sold for $25.00!

Can you imagine the big money spent and made on such books? Making money on a doomsday subject? They even have movies and films promoting a holocaust of the "end of all things!" Suffering! Gloom! Doom! Bloodshed! Wars! Fighting! I can't think of anything more immoral than this — getting wealthy — FAT WEALTHY — over the impending doom of mankind! This scenario no longer fits my newfound and profound optimism for the future of the world. Do as you may — I'm not buying into it! (A little anger there, Oscar? Yes! It bothers me muchly when I see people enslaved into thought systems that are fear-based to motivate you into making them rich! Well, I've gone to preaching again (pontificating). This is supposed to be a book on "hearing from God", but some of what I am saying is what followed — the changes that have taken place since I heard these things. (Is the reader still here?)

Loving Relationships

I think I have learned to love more. Even forgiveness has emerged within me as a crucial importance! I admit there are a few situations where it is extremely difficult to forgive. I am now giving direction to some of the DNA within me to follow what I say! Even though this seemed somewhat ridiculous at first, I have noticed that after a time, a softer and kinder spirit has overcome a rather hard and stormy heart. Yes, I still have a few problems in totally forgiving, but that's "in process!"

While I admit I still have challenges in the area of forgiveness, and I know that this is an absolute must for my own welfare, I do see a much deeper love for all humanity welling up from within. I know what it is — it is the *agape* of God that Paul speaks of in Romans 5:5. So, it is not I but CHRIST of Gal. 2:20. You see, I'm still somewhat Bible-based — a whole lot of somewhat! (That's for you Biblicists! I even have a "connection" with you!)

A New Connectedness

Now that I have mentioned the world connectedness, let me say that that has become a key word in my new vocabulary. I am connected to every living thing and to all non-living things (matter). It is a loving relationship of oneness. It's like family — even including trees... and bumblebees!

Am I trying to sell anything or convince others of my newfound discoveries? Not really — at least not in my conscious thinking (maybe subconsciously!). But I am finding myself with many people along the way of my travels who seem to want to hear what I have to say. Truth has it's own way of promoting itself and getting around!

I do wish for others, and you reading this book, a new freedom in being delivered from the bondage of old worn-out doctrines and belief systems that enslave, into a glorious liberty of being happy and prosperous and enjoying all of what life and God have to offer! Peace, love and joy — and all the rest!

My new experiences resulting from hearing God speak, I guess I ought to label my *after life*! After the old traditions of men! You mean I've died and gone to heaven? Well, yes, sort of! The old "I" died and a new "I" has risen — a living dynamic of the Christ within — but I have not gone to heaven, but heaven has come to me! Now? Yes, now! Right now. I am beginning to realize what it means to be seated with Christ in heavenly places! I am consciously and spiritually ruling and reigning with Christ upon the earth!

Love is being re-affirmed. I already knew this intellectually, as Victor Frankl pointed out, as "discovering the potential in other persons."

How do I explain this new great feeling that I am experiencing? I don't. I can't! It's just there! I love everybody! Almost every thing — with maybe some exceptions: snakes, alligators, gnats and flies!

I love meeting new friends. It's the most exciting part of our travels — sitting around an old campfire! Talking, sharing, singing silly songs and a few serious ones.

In fact, I sense an anointing in R.V. camps around our country. I am beginning to believe that this is one of the places to which He has moved! From "church" buildings to "campsites!" Wow! What a switch! For me, at least!

I see God everywhere! I hear Him in the evening breeze! I love to sit in His presence — watch the clouds roll by — the storm clouds gather. I see His handiwork in the sunsets, a new one every day. I guess I'm beginning to be a mystic! All that word means is mysterious, and will Edna ever agree with that!

Oh, by the way, Edna is going to write a book! She has seen the excitement in me and she gave me the thrilling news just yesterday morning back in Beckley, W.Va. (we're in Charleston as I write this at her sister and brother-in-law, Ruth Anna & Pete Perry's house). Guess what the title is? You guessed it! *"Life with Oscar Poole!"* I can hardly wait to read it!

Well, it's a whole new day for me. "Day," meaning era, or age, or some dimension of time — maybe it's just "NOW" as Echardt Tolle says in his book, *"The Power of Now!"*

More romance in our marriage! Enjoying each other. Great companionship. Holding hands while going down the road in our motorhome! Talking! Singing! Laughing! You will note that this is what I called for in my "Magna Carta", an earlier grandiose reply to God when He asked *"What concerns You?"* It is forthcoming in this little book. It is printed in my earlier book, *Speak-To-It!*

Relationships

This word has become extremely important in my life resulting in "hearing from God!" Especially do I desire helping to heal broken relationships. Rather than setting up walls I want to build bridges! Bridges of love, forgiveness and understanding. I am living in a whole new dimension — ever expanding — that's what the "Kingdom of Heaven" means. Reaching out. Going places. Playing the piano. Sharing. Letting folks know that we care! Doesn't matter where! There are no holy tones! Just plain old casual everyday talking. It's a great way to live! And are we ever enjoying it!

GEN-ius

I am continuing with our discussion on seeking God in a whole new view of everything. Of course, much of this is a continuation of some ideas held before this "exile" period in my life — this decade of listening to the spirit within. It represents tying in some of the old with the new — or you might say, a clearer and newer understanding. This fits in with my understanding already known by me, as progressive revelation — sort of defining and refining previously held views.

But I do think what I now see in regard to genetics ... and certainly with DNA... is a new discovery. I have the feeling that we can give direction to our genetic codes in many areas of our lives. I think some of this is through medicine. I have come to believe that our thoughts and words play an integral role in managing our genes. Yes, I believe DNA can be changed! Probably both ways: from bad to worse, or from good/not-so-good to better.

Many ideas now held by me have come to me through the scientific community (nuclear physics) but as I have explained, I now see no difference between secular and spiritual — or nature and spirit — and this is a new revelation to me, although I had glimpses into this. (This material is covered more in *Speak-To-It!*)

I do know that I have a much improved self-image. When I got into the area of my confessions of faith in my earlier book, there is absolutely no question that this is true! I discovered that through meditation — saying out loud repeatedly — referred to as "spaced repetition" by psychologists, has changed my views about myself and many other things dramatically! Again, this is covered in depth in *Speak-To-It!* I am convinced that we can speak to ourselves, to situations, and circumstances — even to basic matter and effect great changes!

Through this and along with help from others (namely nuclear physicists) I have come to these strongly held views which were not held previously. There seems to be more learning in my seventies (I am 74) than at any other period in my life!

New ideas, some about old things, come to me in rapid succession. It blows my mind! (Spoken metaphorically, although some may interpret it literally! I keep trying to illustrate what's wrong with some of you literal biblicists who interpret the Bible literally, wrongly in my view.)

I find that I am never alone, even in my solitude! I experience sort of an inward fellowship with nature and I guess angels (called as ministering spirits in the Bible), friends who may be a world away, and even sometimes even departed loved ones! I can hear someone reading this book, "There goes Oscar, off the wall again!"

To which I reply, "Off the wall or no wall, I'm only reporting (testifying)."

As I am writing this book, I am asking myself "Why is this — that so many new revelations have and are coming my way?" (A right-now thing!) I think my answer is that I have simply opened myself up to receiving the new now! This goes back to the introduction of *Speak-To-It!* when I discussed who should not read this book! I said, "those who are not open to new understandings of truth!" Seriously.

I think this is the key —openness! Of course, one should not be open to everything that comes along — for there are errors both in fact and judgement amongst us. But, remember, you have a "checks and balances" program within you — it's called conscience, and of course, the Holy Spirit! With the aid of your innate ability that your Creator placed within you, and the Holy Spirit also with you to lead and guide, you can discern between the good and the evil (error and truth), then decide between the two. You will know from within yourself which is true.

We, because of healed broken self-imagery, are transformed (changed) from "can't-doers" to "can-doers." And it surprises us — even astounds us — what we can do! We go ahead and do it! Then back off from it and wonder, "Did that really happen?!"

Along this line I ask the reader to check out for yourself whether the things I say in this book be truth. You have both the responsibility and right to do so. I am not offended at that response. In fact, I am complimented — even at a friendly challenge! Seriously! Please believe me! I genuinely love good, wholesome honest discussions of different perspectives! Seems to me this ought to be fair enough!

I remember well when a certain denominational leader spoke with his compassionate "holy tones" (in 1988) when he declared braggingly that "our denomination" will be the leading denomination by the year 2000! I asked a pastor within that denomination, "Do you think there is room for an alternate view?" I don't recall this friend's response but I do know that it's now 2004 and that silly man's prophecy never came to pass! I knew it wouldn't when I heard it, as I knew that God never rewards such egotistical braggartness!

So it is true with you and me. I expect alternate views! I make no pretense in asserting that I know everything about what I am declaring to be the truth and my new understandings. Remember it is the theme of this book, "when God spoke to me," that I am contending for as the absolute truth, not necessarily what has developed since, these views are certainly open for question! The other is not — they are testimony. I actually heard these messages deep within my being!

Within

This leads me to a brief discussion of a clearer understanding and belief that the Kingdom of God is within! You will notice the many times that "within" appears throughout!

Of course, Jesus taught this back in the first century! So that's not new! It's just that it has come to have a new meaning for me!

I sense or feel this great Kingdom from within myself! All of this "God talk, spirit, thinking, decision-making" is happening within me. I say "big and great!" You cannot measure it! It's a whole new world — all in the Spirit. New perspectives of wholeness, healing, directions, and there is no place where the voice is not heard!

Heaven is now. God is now. He is not a relic, but relevant! You cannot go anyplace where He is not. We find ourselves involved in the creative process! We make things happen! We discover that we are participants in history — affecting great changes — for the better!

CHAPTER VII

"What Concerns You?"

I was walking one of my three-mile walks one day when I was muttering — meditating and saying out loud repeatedly — "The Lord will perfect that which concerns me" (Psalm 138:8). Following one of these repetitions, I heard the voice from inside ask, *"What concerns you?"*

That was back in 1993, 11 years ago. I mention the date because God works through space-time-matter and -motion (Einstein). This is illustrated in nature as seed, time and harvest! When you plant a seed (potential) into the ground, it takes time for it to come into fruition or harvest. This is a spiritual principle in life itself. Another example would be the research scientist who gets an idea which he labels a thesis, then he proceeds to work it out! Yes, time is involved even in the creative process.

In Genesis the creation story is given in time increments of six days. Not literal 24-hour time frames, but much longer duration, that is, according to my view. Even

God had to have time to work things out!

I put together a rather long list of concerns which I began saying back to the personal voice within! Oddly His (God's), First Force (according to Harold Cober), Energy (Einstein) — take your pick! My choice is God! I made this list a part of my daily meditation for the next seven years, and I began to see or realize some of these concerns immediately — as well as a host of them later!

They were practical, everyday things that I really wanted to see happen! I have come to believe that this is spirit-working-out, or manifesting itself, into the world of matter, although I am sure there is a better, scientific way of saying it. A creative process, making itself known into the daily affairs of men! The God-force gently, sometimes in bursts, rising from within (there's that word again).

I am trying to find a simple way to say this! Let us say that it is the Kingdom of God within us, working-out or MAN-ifesting God or Spirit into and through the material world.

One gets an idea. He gets it from within himself. Though the source is not he, it is God — the Divine Force or Spirit. This Divine Force speaks a word or phrase or even a picture or image. We call this in-SPIRIT-ation. I realize that even as I speak this I am writing in mysteries! I am trying to describe the process that seems to be going on within one as an inspirational idea is being birthed within.

When gestation (another metaphor) is complete it is ready to be spoken! When it is spoken (released from the spirit) strange and wonderful things begin to take place! The idea begins to MAN-ifest itself. It begins to take shape (or form). It is beginning to formulate!

The mystery becomes greater as the process continues! Others hear about it through some mysterious connection. God is working to bring this new thing about! It seems like the powers-that-be begin to converge, working in harmonious patterns to cause this (or these) things to happen! But happen it does and the person with the original idea finds that he did not really make this new thing happen although he played a major part in it! He does have the satisfaction that he was the first to know about it! This gives an inward sense of joy and satisfaction that he helped to birth a creative idea! And the more children he has, the happier he gets! (More metaphors — creative ideas, we'll call the next word in this trilogy, "invention" — notice even that word, "IN- [within] VENT- [wind or spirit] ion." A breath of the Spirit within! All seems so simple to me!)

Back to my concerns list. I memorized what concerned me. This was not hard to do because they were for real! They were dreams and aspirations (notice the root word *spirit* again! Everything flows out of the spirit!). I said them aloud, repeatedly until they were almost automatic though they never sounded like merely rote words spoken by a robot. I could sense a wonderful witness on the inside of me as I spoke these concerns. This inside witness is difficult to explain and I think I know partially why — it is beyond the intellect or mind, it is in the Spirit, where sometimes words lose their meaning! I sometimes use the word "feeling" to describe this as contentment, peace, an at-ease-ness, a quietness, a profound satisfaction — but I think that even expressions of emotional feelings are not adequate. Hence I have come to use the word *sense*.

Anyhow, let me say that there is great joy on the inside when you sense the spirit working! I find myself feeling very inadequate trying to describe the workings of the Spirit as they are beyond words, or the intellect. I suppose it's impossible — but you know when it is there! You know, like you have experienced something too great to describe! I believe this happens to all of us!

CHAPTER VIII

"I want you to write it down!"

So, I did. I scratched all of these concerns onto a legal sized paper. Both sides! But that was not enough. I wrote down more concerns, things I wanted to see come about in my life — many times I thought it was too late, since I had finished my professional preaching career. Little did I realize that with God time was of little significance! What I was about to witness was the unfolding of a miracle! Only the form was about to change. From a building with a steeple on it — looking up — to one with a pig on it — looking out. Little did I realize that many of the dreams and visions I had carried with me since childhood were about to take place! Not through a church, but through a roadside business. And a tacky one at that!

I named my concern list my "Magna Carta." After much usage the pages were tearing and the edges wearing off so I decided that if they were to last I had better place them in our safety deposit box at the bank. This I did and there they lie for our posterity — this is the value I place upon them!

I say "Magna Carta" because it seemed to me it became a document that laid out sort of a blue print for the remaining years of my life — although I was just getting started in a new career at age 59! Well, I thought of Col. Sanders of fried chicken fame. He was 65 when he hit the road with a sack of flower in the back of his '46 Ford! So, at least I had a six-year jump on him!

I have made some copies of my Magna Carta and I am going to print one right here in this book! It does not resemble the rag-tag original in the safety box, for after all it is a copy. Further, it is at points, a paraphrase of the original, but in essence it is a duplicate of the original.

I need to mention about a scripture that came alive in all this! This is another example of a rhema word — a scripture made alive — that I mentioned earlier. It is Habbakuk 3:1-3, when the prophet declared, *"Write the vision, make it plain upon tablets, so he who sees it may run with it!"*

Let me explain that the original word that I heard within myself was not a coming alive of this scripture. Rather, it was a direct voice spoken directly to me in a distinct clear voice — the one I had heard many times before! The scripture here given is merely an affirmation of what

I had heard directly! My conclusion? I'm not the only one to whom God had spoken these words!

This has two effects upon me. It prevents me from a "cocky" attitude — that I am above or superior to someone else — but it makes me feel that I am included in very good company! He speaks like this to all — He is no respecter of persons — to you and me. I don't think you have to hear a voice to write down your dreams, concerns and goals. Just do it! About every self-improvement psychologist I know of agrees that we should write down our goals.

I don't like the word "secular," as I believe all is spiritual — but for the sake of explanation I will use it here. Modern secular psychology agrees with scriptural declarations, and why not? If you get your historical perspective focused clearly you will know that it was theology that gave birth to science. Truths in science — in this case, psychology — merely affirm truths in the Bible or elsewhere, as truth begets truth and remains truth no matter where it is and in whatever form it appears!

My Magna Carta

"The Lord will perfect that which concerns me" (Psalm 138:8). I added *"and is perfecting,"* as I understand God works through time, matter, space and at a certain speed (Einstein).

"La Vie in Georgia, an international retreat center." (La Vie now sits on 12 acres of choice north Georgia moun-

tain land given to me, is incorporated and I am president of it.)

"Car tags from all over the United States, Canada, Mexico and many foreign countries. A great gathering or coming together.

"Hand clap offerings. Anointings.

"Orchestras, trumpets, bugles, pianos, organs, flutes, marching bands, tambourines.

"A TALL TOWER (building) with a chapel and office on top for PERSPECTIVE.

"Expectancy. Great numbers. Positive faith. Excitement. Enthusiasm. Youth. Children. Senior citizens (I now am one!). Good will.

"Vision. 'Writing and running with it!' (I write the vision, the people — thousands — run with it. They tell it while I sleep!)

"Books, booklets (this is one of them), pamphlets, newsletters, newspapers, cassette tapes, T.V. exposure (so many times I have lost track!), radio network (all over the world), magazines."

*Note: When the Pig-Hill-of-Fame was birthed I simply thought of it as a part of this "writing the vision!" Anyhow, the people run with it, and thousands run to it!

"Entertaining groups. Playing the piano. (Wherever our motorhome goes, this occurs!)

"Travel. Much by car, jet, and by bus. (I guess the R.V. is the bus. It is a class A and looks like one.)

"Retreats. Seminars. Celebrations. Rallies.

"RESPECT. Amongst my peers and the Christian world.

"WEALTH, RICHES & HONOR in my household. House bought and paid for. (It was debt free the day we moved into it.) Retirement secure. The knowledge of witty inventions.

"Super great favor with God and man.

"Super abundance of wealth to establish God's covenant.

"Good food for Edna and me, at home and eating in fine restaurants. (Although I now prefer eating in the hole-in-the wall places!)

"Mingling and meeting professional people — doctors, attorneys, dentists, educators, governors, presidents and their wives, judges, senators, statesmen, dignitaries, and uncommon common people.

"Good clothes for Edna, me, our children, and our seeds' seed perpetually.

"Good HEALTH for Edna, me, our children, and our seeds' seed perpetually.

"Two-tone blue Cadillac bought and paid for. (We now own two Cadillacs but neither one of them is blue!)

"All the fruit of the Spirit. Love, Peace. Joy. Happiness.

"Prosperity. Success. Achievement. For God's glory. To tell others so they can be healed, set free, and become "plantings of the Lord."

"Hallelujah! Praise the Most High God! Through the SPIRIT! (Note the praising and thanksgiving twenty (20) years before the manifestation! This illustrates that God, the Eternal Constant, operates or brings into actualization, through time-space-matter-motion — Einsteinian!)

"Beautiful relationships within the family and in-laws. (Some of this is in PROCESS!)

"Romance in our marriage. Enjoyment of each other.

"In the NAME of Jesus Christ. (I have since added "Yahweh, Spirit, the I AM ... total DEITY).

"Thank you Father, for bringing all this ... and more to pass!"

The above "Magna Carta" as I said earlier, became sort of a blue print or guide for the years that have followed! Life has seemed to be an outward flow of these concerns spoken out loud repeatedly (see *Speak-To-It!* for a more detailed account on meditation).

Not all of these dreams have been accomplished or fulfilled, but most of them have come to pass! Especially is this true in associations with "statesmen, educators, doctors, governors," "great numbers," "books, booklets, cassette tapes, T.V. exposure, radio networks, magazines," "much travel," "Respect," "Super great favor," "Good health for Edna and me," "Prosperity, Success, Achievement," ... all this and more!

And it seems like every day the abundance of this increases. Of course, the form of our life's fulfillment has changed from a church building to a BAR-B-Q building. Do you think that I restricted the flow of God's success through us by limiting God in the old churchy form? I wonder! I do not really know but I can't help but think about it. We did well while in the church syndrome. In fact, I loved much of it ... the preaching, interpersonal relationships, and the changing of lives. But the same has and is happening through this very different form which has become my forum. I speak to quite large rallies, one-on-one relationships, counseling, write books, play the piano, teach seminars and all the rest of the good stuff without the old boring board meetings, church fusses, negative programs, etc. Now it's all positive atmosphere, almost totally.

There is great joy amongst us as much of what we do is termed "silly." PIG-MOBY-IL, TAJ-MA-HOG, HOG ROCK CAFE, and the PIG-HILL-OF-FAME! Families gather. People laugh. The atmosphere itself draws people in and many say their lives have changed for the better.

The people return and an expanding family atmosphere dominates! You can sense or feel it!

All because we had the vision, thought it, talked it. Every time the vision or idea is spoken, more happens! You see it's not just the original thinking and speaking — it's the continued speaking by the hundreds and thousands that have become involved. This, I think, has much to do with the exponentiality of our growth! Others working with you.

Keep in mind the Magna Carta was simply the "writing down" in a response to the question of deity (God) into the inner being of one person, me. It has been nothing less that a thrill to see this thing unfold — still in process!

Do you have a Magna Carta for your life?

CHAPTER IX

"Jarrell is going to give you that land for your retreat!"

This chapter backs up a bit from the above discussion. The time was shortly before the BAR-B-Q saga began, in 1988 when we were living in Mineral Bluff, Ga. Where *La Vie*, our mountain retreat, now stands, a converted barn with a rock fireplace, a mountain stream, a meadow, a place to park motorhomes, and room for a new lodge — you know, that place where God seems to talk that I mentioned earlier?

I shall never forget the day that God spoke to me about Jarrell giving 12½ acres of beautiful mountain land to us! It was a Monday morning at 7 a.m. when Jarrell Anderson called. Jarrell and his wife, Mary, were developing one hundred acres of land for homesites near Mineral Bluff on Piney Mountain. In his slow, deep voice he said, "Oscar, I want to talk with you!"

I asked myself what I had done wrong... Isn't it strange that many of our responses to even good things are framed in some sort of a negative manner?

I told Jarrell that I was leaving immediately for the dentist's office over in Chatsworth to do a root canal, and I'd had a severe toothache all weekend.

"Well," said Jarrell, "how about meeting Mary and me at the Fannin Inn for lunch upon your return?"

"Okay," I said. "Is 11 o'clock alright?"

"Yes," he said. "Mary and I will meet you at the Fannin Inn at 11 o'clock!"

I was puzzled. What did Jarrell want with me? Why is he bringing Mary with him and why did he ask that I bring Edna along? These and other thoughts ran through my mind.

Just outside Ellijay, on Hwy. 282, between Ellijay and Chatsworth, God spoke! (When God speaks, it's hard to forget the time and place!) That inner voice — loud, distinct, clear — out of the blue... *"Jarrell wants to give you that land for the retreat!"* That's exactly what I heard.

"Oh, no," I replied. "He's not going to do that!" (Notice my negative response!) Maybe I was shocked in disbelief — it's one of those too good to be true deals!

God's reply, *"Yes, he is. He's going to give you that land!"*

"Aw, no, he's not!" Here I go again with my great faith, a man of the cloth, a minister, one who preaches faith— I can't believe what I am hearing!

So I went off to Chatsworth and all the while the dentist is working on my tooth this matter is on my mind!

A couple of hours later, now 10 a.m., I am returning home on the same highway and almost at the same place, I heard God's voice again! *"Yes, Jarrell is going to give you that land!"* This time, the third time, I did not reply. I was beginning to believe that what I had heard might be true!

So, we all, Edna, Mary, Jarrell and I, met at the Fannin Inn, ate a nice lunch, had a pleasant conversation and left for our home back out toward Mineral Bluff — not a word about any land being given. We had never discussed a single time about having a retreat on the property, although I'm sure he had heard me talk about having a retreat center.

We drove into the front yard, Edna and I, in our white Chevette and Jarrell and Mary in his black Bronco. We all got out and gathered around the front hood of his Bronco. Jarrell reached for a large, rolled up document, opened it to the survey page of the property and said, "Mary and I want to give you the property for your retreat!"

Do you have any idea of how I must have felt? Well, I should not have been surprised — God had told me three times!

Does God speak today?! You tell me!

CHAPTER X

A Couple of Other Times God Spoke

Again, this chapter goes back to a few years earlier during our moving to North Carolina. As you can see, preachers are constantly on the move — especially this one!

We were just approaching the state line, still in South Carolina — that place where the "Pedro" thing is. (Again, you can't forget the time and place God speaks!)

All of a sudden I felt a strange, heavy feeling in the lower part of my stomach. Something was wrong!

Here we were, almost to our destination, Fayetteville, N.C., only about 50 miles away. We were happy and excited as we were responding to the Bishop, our personal friend, to become the pastor of this rather run down congregation.

When into my mind, flashed the picture of a note

on the front door of the parsonage, just an hour away, that read, "DO NOT ENTER."

I did not know what to make of this but there it was — a vision with no voice.

Shortly, we arrived at our destination. We parked out front, walked up to the front door and, you guessed it, there was a handwritten note on the door which read, in essence, "DO NOT ENTER — until you call this number."

I found a phone and called the number. The lady, a church member, told me that the church board met three days earlier, had a fight over my bringing a concert piano into their sanctuary, and left instructions for me not to unload it!

I called the district superintendent who knew nothing about it. After a rather long discussion we decided to unload and he said, "go ahead and put the piano where you need to." Edna and I had talked that we might just drive on — to where I do not know!

To shorten the story, we went to work in our new somewhat dissent-ridden congregation. Within two months a small group of about 10 people left the church, leaving 20 members still attending. Within 24 months, the church grew from 37 to over 200 — then new problems arose and that's another story! I might mention that the yearly budget grew from $17,000 to over $100,000.

This episode of the vision at the North Carolina/

South Carolina border is not given to say that "God spoke," but I think it is of such interest to include in this little book. Some might call this a word of knowledge, from the Spirit within. I'll let the reader decide!

Another scenario occurred 69 years ago when I was five years of age. It was in New Smyrna Beach, Fla., the place of my birth — the origin of this part of the species!

This is not a "God speaking to me" event (I don't think), but rather a vision that has stayed with me all these years. All this was within me at, I repeat, the age of five! I never told a single person about this for at least twenty years as I was simply afraid to share it with anyone. In fact, I have not told this to many people until now. Here it is, turned loose in this book forum and I will close out this essay on *"God in the Marketplace!"*

This vision occurred in dreams — at this innocent tender age. It happened over and over until it was indelibly implanted into my permanent psyche and I could see the vision even during the day! I must confess that I still see this even as I write these words on a cold, damp, rainy day here in Hurricane, W.Va., at the home of Glen and Peggy Morton, so real and plain to me that I want to ask if you see it!

There it is! A vast sea of faces, as far as the eye can see, of people — all gathered into one place. You cannot count them! As far as you can see this throng of people fades into the distance like an infinitum of seeing. I have always wondered what it is!

It is a gathering, or coming together of people! Is this the family of God gathering together? Is this a part of the "every man shall know me — from the least to the greatest?" What is it? My best guess is that it is the whole world — I have no way of counting them! Is this God drawing all men unto Himself? This represents the best answer I can give to my own question! But the vision is still there! Unimpaired after nearly 70 years! I would like to believe that this really is in fact, God's people coming together. I certainly hope so and I want to have my part in it!

CHAPTER XI

A New Awareness Emerging

A new awareness is emerging all around us. All nature is singing the one-song of the universe! More persons are hearing it! In spite of apparent evils — and there are crucial ones — there is a coming together of persons. A critical mass is gaining momentum! Optimism is beginning to abound!

Critical Mass

What do we mean by critical mass? When enough people sense this new awakening the new awareness of God's presence will have great effect. Progressive change is becoming the order for many! Positive mental attitudes are developing. Mind sets of peace and goodwill are beginning to abound! You can see it! You can sense it! You can feel it in the air! People are learning that love conquers all! That the Spirit is for real — that the Kingdom of

God is now and is amongst us!

How many is enough people experiencing this new wave and effect great change? Not many! Just how many remains a mystery. Only God knows! As in the Bible, when one put a thousand to flight, two can put 10,000, and when you get to eight it is one billion. Of course there is strength in numbers, but as has been said, "One plus God equals a majority!"

This new awareness is growing, and rapidly. All we have to do is open our hearts and let the light in! This new light is shining, right now, over each person, home, or "stable!" It's messengers and messages are for good — for all — no respecter of persons! It's a realizing of connectedness — that we are all connected to each other — to nature, things (matter) and the created order.

This light has been shining since the time of Isaiah! It never quits burning. Peace on earth, good will to men HAS TO BE! Its instigator is God. He has never lost a battle and somehow (I don't know how) this great Kingdom of God shall reign mightily over the earth, and best of all, God is not only with and amongst us, He is in us!

Right Here ... Now ... Relevant

God is not only out there — He is right here, and now! Relevant in every conceivable way. Expansion is its very nature. People are hearing God directly — each man for himself! I can't find enough positive words to describe it! Darkness and all that it stands for, is being overcome by this light that is shining "o'er all the earth!"

More people are seeing themselves as God sees them! Positive, whole, healed, set-free, as He is so are we! Creative imagery surrounds us! More are tapping into it and drawing from it! Our very DNA is responding to this call! Genes, electrons, neutrons, nuclei, molecules are hearing! Great mysteries of yesteryear are becoming commonplace though we be awestruck as one mystery unfolds after another! God (deity) is gaining in rapidity as He reveals Himself exponentially in progressive revelation.

The old is giving way to the new! We are witnessing new heavens and a new earth right before our very eyes!

A theology of hope, lost for a time, is returning. Despair is losing its grip as one new discovery after another takes place.

We are returning to nature — to our original home — surroundings of love and peace — where we can hear God more clearly and fully!

God lives here! This is "My Father's World!" We can see Him everywhere and His goodness abounds! Rebellion and resistance are crumbling, submission is increasing to God's ways! Nature is joined to Spirit. Oneness is here!

Have you seen the picture of the earth from the spacecraft Hubbell, looking back at the earth? It resembles an eye — the eye of God! You can see emanations of God — God in people, giving off auras of God's presence! Yes! This is God's home. He has brought heaven to earth! He is here amongst us in the now — and are we most privileged!

It's a new day! A new era! When the disciples asked Jesus when the end of the age (not world as in "earth") would come about, he informed them that they, this generation, would not pass until those things of which they spoke would be fulfilled.

So that age came to an end. A new one began. Now it has ended. Another new age has begun! It's new and now. Let's enjoy it!

ADDENDUM I

New Insights Gained from Listening

The following is a partial list of new insights or revealed truths received during the years following 1988.

1. Basic matter seems to have the capacity to respond to a loving person!
2. If it's new, it's now and if it's now, it's new — never having been done before!
3. Matter (nature) is "spirit slowed down to visibility."
4. We, as spirit-beings, are connected into both nature and spirit.
5. The created order is in pain, waiting for us to manifest healing and wholeness.
6. We can see and do as God sees and does!
7. We are surrounded by creativity that can be

tapped into for the asking. We are submerged into this creativity.

8. We can call things that "ARE NOT" AS IF they were, until they BECOME! We are co-creators with God!

9. Infinite wisdom is available to us!

10. Common or average persons can become uncommon or above average when inspired or enlivened by the Spirit!

11. A special relationship exists between us and all that surrounds us — persons and nature!

12. Love — God's kind (agape-nature) fills our natures.

13. As God is — so are we!

14. Now!

15. Eternity is now (tomorrow will be another now). Live in it!

16. Truth is revealed progressively, dependent only upon our ability to receive it.

17. It is spirit-over-mind-over-matter.

18. Genes (as in DNA) can be affected, given direction, or changed.

19. This is a new day, era, or age.

20. Loving optimism changes pessimism or negativism.

21. Right will win over wrong or evil.

22. Science is a friend to theology.

23. The world of spirit is vast and unexplored.

24. Imagination (ability to see) determines what we can do!

25. Our self-image determines the extent of goals.

26. What the mind can conceive, and the heart believe, we can achieve! (CBA)

27. I'm not what I think I am, I'm not what you think I am, but I am what I think you think I am!

28. Love is the commitment to helping discover the potential in others. (Frankl)

29. God (Spirit, Deity, Energy) is the ultimate constant but works progressively through space-time-matter-motion. (Einstein)

30. Peace and good will shall cover the earth!

31. We can heal and restore the created order by speaking-to-it!

32. Theology, philosophy, and nuclear physiology are connected together in a harmonious relationship!

33. Matter can be filled with spirit — sick and rebellious cells can respond to calls of loving correction!

34. Physical immune systems can be strengthened or enhanced by our words, actions and by medicine (holistic).

35. Our immune systems are strengthened when we affirm or strengthen others!

36. We can find ourselves again!

37. Evil cannot triumph over God!

38. Essence is more important than form!

39. Growth, expandability, is the nature of the world of spirit.

40. Exponentiality is God's way of expanding.

41. The secret of the uni-verse is a person.

42. Reality is comprised of loving relationships!

43. Legalism destroys the spirit! It negates the truth and stifles creativity!

44. Complaining and criticizing weakens immune systems, slows down creativity and destroys loving relationships.

45. There is a correct time to reveal secrets. A new revelation should be held in secret until its time comes to reveal it!

46. Getting up early is an important factor in success.

47. Success is achieving your goals.

48. A wise person is open for correction.

49. Visions and goals should be written!

50. Living creatively is enjoyable! It makes even hard work fun.

51. Listening is a fine art and must be planned and learned.

52. Truth, the ultimate constant, does not change — but our understandings do.

53. Open minds open the spirit! The choice is ours!

54. Humility, patience and lovingkindness are absolute necessities for progressive journeys of faith.

55. Becoming a genius is not necessarily determined by heredity or environment. It can sometimes be discovered! (Rhine)

56. Man is a sleeping giant waiting to be awakened.

ADDENDUM II

The Republican National Convention, 2004 New York City

I have decided to include this report of Edna's and my attendance at the 2004 RNC as I think this experience is a culmination of hearing from God, and a natural but spiritual consequence to hearing that voice within, which I call God. The event itself is so overwhelming that I believe it is a fitting climax to *"God in the Marketplace!"*

A Year Earlier

Sometime during 2003 there developed within me the thought or conviction that I should attend all the republican conventions of 2004 and that I should build the schedule of my year around them. I am not saying that God told me this, but that this arose within my spirit.

So, March 2004 came and I attended the Gilmer County Convention and was elected as a delegate to both the 10th District Georgia Convention held in Northwest Georgia in April, and the State Convention held in Columbus in May. This growing conviction became so strong within me that Edna and I had two tailor-made bright yellow suits made for these events, at a cost of several hundred dollars!

Disappointed

I tried to have myself elected from both the district and state convention levels to be a delegate to the national convention just concluded, August 28 through September 2, 2004. I could not get myself elected as either a delegate or alternate — and further, I sensed there was somebody who did not favor my going to the convention. I have a real gift for sensing when something is wrong, but I wrestled with this idea that maybe it was a little paranoia. Anyhow, I began to sense some rejection.

Oh, by the way, way down in Columbus, I was the only delegate whose picture appeared on the front page of the Columbus paper on Saturday morning, and one of the few seen on local television the night before! Could there be a little jealousy amongst some of us? Yes, that thought ran through my mind.

I began to have some doubts about going to New

York City. But a real saint entered my life once again — I speak of Carolyn Meadows, our Republican National Committee Woman. She said to me, "I want you and Edna to go as my guests!"

But then I pondered all the terrorist threats being made about disrupting the upcoming national process, and I wasn't a delegate. So I wrestled further with the idea of whether to go.

The invitation forms arrived, Edna and I filled them out and gave the state headquarters our visa number and waited. Two months passed and we had heard nothing. This added to my concern of spending all that money and then going up there and perhaps staying in the hotel!

I prayed. I asked God out loud — "Do you want me to go?" No answer. Then I said, "If you don't want me to go please stop, put a block in my path so I'll know!" I am revealing this personal struggle about hearing from God to let you know that it's not always easy to hear God speak! Since no stumbling block occurred, we packed our bags and left for New York City based upon the lack of a hindrance plus the earlier conviction of 2003.

The Atlanta Airport

We arrived at the Atlanta airport. I was feeling somewhat freer in my spirit and beginning to feel the excitement that was on the way. I met DeVida, an official with Air Tran Airways who was about to leave for the day and had in her hand a book about God. To make a longer story shorter I told her that I had just written a book, *Speak-To-It!* and autographed her a copy. Connection! We immediately connected in our spirits and we had a time together! She even told me the flights were over-booked, and this led to our giving up our seats and departing three hours later. The airline gave us two round trip passes to as far away as Los Angeles. It just happens that Edna and I want to go back to see our friends in San Diego — only this time mostly free!

So, I think to myself, now I have two affirmations that this is a "right" trip. I feel a littler freer! You see, the answer to my question about going is coming in stages — not simple, clear cut as at other times.

Arrival

New York City?! We arrived there in good shape and within two hours were all set up in the fabulous Ritz-Carlton hotel in the southern financial district of Manhattan. Our fifth floor room overlooked the Statue of Liberty!

For the next five days we "wined and dined" with top officials of Georgia — the governor, senators, congressmen, their wives (specifically Nancy Coverdell and

Leslie Mattingly), party officials and many others. At this point I invite the reader to turn back to the earlier section of this book, my Magna Carta, and simply make the connections with what I said years ago and what is taking place now, about presidents, governors and their wives!

Orientation

An orientation meeting was held for all delegates, alternates and guests (that's us — Oscar & Edna). Somehow there emerged a feeling of acceptance — that we're all Georgians — here to represent Georgia together. Let me give credit to Alec Poitevant, our state GOP president. He made us all, guests included, feel like family. I have to say, "Thank you, Alec!"

All during this time we are meeting new friends. People we'd never known all of a sudden becoming connected and life-long friends. Expansion!

We all, over 300 of us, went to see a Broadway play, *"The Beauty and the Beast!"* What a thrill. One happy family from Georgia experiencing this moving play of how love changed a beast into a prince! So, the whole RNC starts out on a spiritual note!

Let me say parenthetically that while Edna and I were promised one pass to one session, we actually received all five passes to all five sessions! See my affirmation of faith in my earlier book, *Speak-To-It!* on "I have super great favor with both God and man!" This said twenty years earlier!

Why did we go to the RNC?

Every event needs a purpose — a reason or reasons.

First, the one year earlier conviction that I should attend the '04 national convention. That's enough reason! That, I take to be of God!

But I have others. I asked myself why I should go, and here's what I came up with:

Number one, I wanted to represent my state of Georgia — to be sort of a goodwill ambassador for my state, like my mayor, Mack West, says I am for our little town of East Ellijay!

Number two, I wanted to make more friends and "love on" more people! I am a people-person and I have within me a profound love for people.

Number three, I wanted to speak to the issues! This I did on network television (U.S., Europe, Far East, and Mid-East)! Think about it! A small businessman, an entrepreneur representing all the other entrepreneurs from a small town, U.S.A., speaking to world issues!

The Yellow Suit

Number four, Edna and I wanted to make a statement of joy by wearing our bright yellow suits! To let folks know that involvement in politics could and should be an enjoyable experience — that one can laugh and have fun while at the same time dealing with survival issues. You see, I believe that each of us gives off emanations, vibrations, auras, that we have a presence and this presence either attracts or detracts. We found that its probably 100 to one on the attraction. Even "liberals" liked us!

Number five, we certainly desired to make media coverage and this we did — probably 200 medias! I will try to list the ones that I know first-hand.

Media List

1. First and foremost was the live CNN moment when I was the first person to greet former president George Bush and Barbara Bush as they entered the floor! Wow! Thrill! An eternal moment, with a brief chat. Live national T.V.!

2. The AP (Associated Press). I am listing these in priority fashion in terms of my thinking. Their photo of me with David Barbee, a delegate from Augusta, Ga., was covered by hundreds of newspapers throughout the U.S. and Canada — I don't know where else. Harold Shock sent me one from Thunder Bay, Canada (Gerald Scott) and another from Anchorage, Alaska. Front full page — in color!

3. Fox 5 in Atlanta. They even covered me playing the piano at the Ritz-Carlton, plus addressing my admiration for Zell Miller!

4. WSB-TV, Channel 2, Atlanta, carried me on the evening news endorsing Zell Miller. This according to Larry Rice.

5. TV-46 (CBS) in Atlanta.

6. ABC Evening News with Peter Jennings, report from Glen & Peggy Morgan.

7. David Letterman Show, CBS, etc. They were sort-of making fun! But who cares?! Didn't I mention that we were there to have fun?!

6. 60 Minutes, CBS. Third Day, a contemporary Christian Music group from Marietta, Ga., and frequent guests at our BAR-B-Q restaurant, was filmed at our Georgia delegation site, and I happened to be the only one sitting there. The rest were all at a meeting and I, being only a guest, was seated there and the producer asked me if it was okay to use the Georgia sign as a backdrop and I said "Yes!" They allowed me to be a part of the backdrop!

7. MSNBC-TV, report from Pete and Ruth Anna Perry.

8. The Internet — who knows at the millions of people who saw us there?

9. The *New York Times* wire service showing a great shot of Edna and me with the whole Madison Square

Garden with all its festive regalia in the background. This was the front page full-color of the Anchorage newspaper and hundreds of others!

10. Several New York City television stations.

11. The *New York Post* — full picture of Edna and me, a couple at the LeGuardia Airport said, "You're in today's paper!"

12. Other medias known by me firsthand: Minneapolis TV, with one of their senators, Alabama TV with Senator Shelby, *Augusta Chronicle, Atlanta Journal-Constitution,* Fox-Houston (a note from Dorothy Halstead), the hundreds of individual photos, perhaps a thousand — returning to their hometowns across America and I'm sure many of them finding themselves in local small town newspapers.

All of the above list are media that I know firsthand!

Other media that I remember talking to and being covered by, although I have no idea what they did with it, include UPI, BBC-London, PBSA, Berlin TV, two newspapers in Amsterdam, Swiss TV, Madrid TV, Jerusalem TV, Taiwan TV, *New York Times,* C-Span, *Time Magazine, Newsweek Magazine,* Washington D.C. radio, and Al-Jazera TV (that was a "scary" one and you had better believe that after their interview I carefully tried to remember what I had said and hoped I had used good diplomacy). Anyhow, imagine the very possibility of the people in Iraq, Iran, Syria and Saudi Arabia listening to and watching a man in a yellow suit with an American patriotic hat!

Number six: Lastly, regarding why did we go? I suppose it might be to increase our BAR-B-Q business back home in Georgia! I'm sure that's in there somewhere, but you see where I placed it — last. I appreciate our business and of course want to grow, but we have all we need. But growth and expansion are, after all, a part of my theology! But in my heart the other five reasons are far more important.

The Bus Trip

I must include this! It was the second day of the convention. All the Georgia delegation had gone across town to a meeting. Edna and I in our yellow suits, got ourselves ready by 3:30 p.m. (I mention the time because it was important to what I am about to reveal.)

The buses started to run at 4 p.m., but somehow they loaded Edna and me onto a bus and took off — headed to Madison Square Garden. A delegate had loaned me his floor pass, which was good until 8 p.m. We arrived at MSG at 4 p.m. and we were able to spend the next four hours on the floor of the convention! Keep in mind this amount of time is almost unheard of and after all, we were only "guests!"

During these four hours I experienced a media blitz! I say "I" because Edna got tired and went back to our seats to rest while I "made the rounds." I tried to count the media in my mind and I lost track after about 25 or 30! I believe I am safe in saying that it was 50 or more! And this only during one session!

It was during this floor experience that I was greeted by Mayor Bloomberg, who personally welcomed me to New York City! Pretty "high cotton," wouldn't you say?

But the highlight I am trying to describe here is the bus trip itself! Here were Edna and I, the only two on the bus, with the driver and a police escort. This was a spiritual moment I'll never forget! Edna and I escorted on a half million dollar bus, our own private driver and our own NYPD escort! How could I believe this! We drove through and around police barricades, past a few protesters — right to Madison Square Garden!

The point I really want to get to is about half way to the convention center the thought came to me, "I'll move heaven and earth for someone who is flowing with me — past terrorists, protestors, blocked streets..." This in New York City! I will never forget the moments on this bus trip! Never!

I think I ought to include that in my Magna Carta, I "spoke" of much travel by car, jet and by bus! I'm telling you — there's something to this speaking-to-it!

Some Concluding Observations

There are so many so I will make them in list fashion.

1. Edna and I experienced an awesomeness to the whole experience.

2. We felt a part of a right-now event!

3. The entire process was a challenge for us. From some early apprehension to relief when it was over! I am referring mainly to security.

4. The events — as they unfolded, proved that my one year earlier feeling that we should attend was correct — that I had "heard from God" in my spirit!

5. I witnessed the power of imagery time after time, right before my very eyes!

6. Spiritual attraction was at work! I am convinced it was not just the yellow suits — but we had something to say — and the media listened!

7. I learned there is still a place for the "little guy" in the Republican party. It has helped me to distinguish between a populist (that's me, a person of the people — and the fat-cat elitist, and we have both amongst us! So, I am admitting there is some division in our Republican ranks and this needs to change!

8. I have come to understand my own political stance much better! I certainly am not a "left-wing-socialist-radical" — nor am I a "far-right-ultra-conservative"

with no common sense values. I see myself as somewhat a "centrist," with neither extreme. I'm not sure I like the term "moderate" but that might describe me partly! Too big a subject to discuss at length here!

Let me conclude by referring back to my Magna Carta one last time, when I heard God say within my spirit, *"If you'll get on the side of that hill and do the menial work, I'll show the world what I will do!"*

Well, that's been fifteen years ago and I think that attending the RNC in NYC August 28 through September 2, 2004, represents quite a culmination of what God said to me many years before!

And after all, this is a book about *"God in the Marketplace,"* and I have sought to relate how the marketplace was the natural and spiritual workings-out of what I heard! I can make no other conclusion!

I hope I have demonstrated how theology and the everyday marketplace connect!

—Col. Oscar Poole

ADDENDUM III

∽

Secrets of Success

The following material is what I call my "Secrets of Success." They are taken from a video tape, "Col. Poole's Secret Recipe for Success," a professional television interview with talk-show host Joe McCutchen.

These are statements of philosophy and practical suggestions for achieving ones goals.

1. Tap into your DIVINE CONNECTION.
2. CONTAGION! Allow these divine auras to emanate.
3. VISION. It is progressive and you must have it! You must "see" yourself as successful!
4. IMAGERY. What you can SEE and BELIEVE, you can ACHIEVE.
5. SELF-TALK. This releases creative energy and gives direction.
6. Do enough RIGHT things and BREAKS will come

your way.

7. BE UNIQUE. In our case it was the PIG-MOBY-IL, the PIG-HILL-OF-FAME, et. al.

8. It's easier to receive forgiveness than permission!

9. WORK, WORK WORK!

10. Maintain a LOW OVERHEAD.

11. Be FRIENDLY! Smile.

12. The customer comes FIRST.

13. Make free use of the MEDIA. Ours began with "call-in" radio talk shows.

14. Never be ashamed of your POLITICAL STANCE.

15. Stay FOCUSED on your goals.

16. Re-adjust goals.

17. WRITE your goals.

18. Repeat POSITIVE personal declarations of faith. Daily.

19. Food QUALITY consistently excellent.

20. Dare to believe even though in a business recession (we began during one in 1989).

21. Willingness to be laughed at! We were!

22. INVOLVE customers ideas.

23. Have something like a PIG-MOBY-IL.

24. Keep it SIMPLE.

25. We were "so tacky, it's classic!" (Swedish Embassy)

26. Develop a TEAM SPIRIT.

28. Have FUN!

29. Believe and practice EXPONENTIALITY!

30. "Hang around at the top." (Steve Spurier)

31. Be CONSISTENT.

32. LOCATION, LOCATION, LOCATION!

33. VISIBILITY.

34. ACCESSIBILITY.

35. Receive CORRECTION.

36. Maintain a healthy exercise program.

37. PRAISE and AFFIRM others.

38. Keep the POWER OF THE SECRET!

39. Adequate parking.

40. Have three or four trusted COUNSELORS.

41. ASK for help.

42. Have at least one JOE McCUTCHEN as your friend.

43. CREATIVITY EXPANDS, GROWS, <u>AS</u> you move toward your goals.

44. Have a DAPDAE system:

    D – Data

    A – Analyze the data

    P – Plan

    D – Delegate

    A – Action

    E – Evaluate

45. Every time you set a new goal you create a situation for some creative TENSION and CONFLICT.

46. GIVE THANKS — OFTEN! In fact, overdo it!

47. SPEAK-TO-IT! Matter and situations.

48. Sacrifice pleasure for capital outlay; e.g., money spent on cars, invest in property.

49. One success leads to another. You can develop a "habit of success!" (Schuller)

50. Learn to "point!" (Delegate – inspiration from Glen Bowen's father.)

51. Take a trip and "think" about it! (Detachment)

52. Allow your healthy PERSONA to develop (a loving presence).

53. Daring to do the IMPOSSIBLE is an ACT OF FAITH!

54. See PROCESS as a goal. Make they journey a success itself.

55. Allow NEW IDEAS to come your way and be open to the "good" ones.

56. Again, LISTEN to that voice within and to others.

57. Live in the NOW!

58. Learn how to BREATHE! Inhaling and exhaling can be a refreshing experience.

59. DO NOT SUCCUMB to an elitist attitude.

60. Stay HUMBLE!

61. Don't forget where you came from!

62. Or, the ones who helped you get where you are!

63. DANCE to the rhythms you hear INSIDE!

64. REST daily. Take breaks, naps.

65. REJOICE AND BE GLAD!

66. Then WRITE about it! Who knows, you might become a writer!

How To Listen

This little book, *"God in the Marketplace,"* has been written about when God spoke to me! It concludes by asking, "What has He told *you*?!" It has been the theme of this material that the universe is understood in personal relationships — that even nature is related to us — and that we are connected to all things animate or inanimate. This makes for excited living! We talk or converse with one another. So, it is not so far-fetched that God speaks today!

"But," you might say, "I've never heard God speak!" Have you listened? Or have you ever thought about it? Certainly, if you have been taught that He doesn't, you probably have not heard His voice, as listening to the inner voice requires a mind-set for listening. So, start thinking about it!

Other Voices

There are other voices that you will discover —

even in your stillness — so you must discern amongst them which is the voice of God. Stored in your memory bank are voices from your past that are simply that — memories!

But, when God speaks you will know it! It's like when you experience an earthquake — somehow you just know it! No one has to tell you. Your Creator has made you that way. He created you to have fellowship with Him and that includes talking.

Turn off the radio!

Most people that I know leave the radio on everywhere they drive their cars! As soon as the switch is turned on here comes that blasting noise! Most folks play it loud! Even so-called "Christian music" fills the surrounding air waves. Who could ever hear God, or anyone else for that matter, over and above the noise? It's almost like we can't stand stillness and quietness. I must admit there is some music that is soothing and creates an atmosphere for listening for God to speak, but that has not been the emphasis of this book.

What I am maintaining is that in the natural course of casual every day living, *God speaks within us* about situations, dangers that confront us, decisions we face, business matters — just ordinary, and certainly the not-so-ordinary, day-to-day stuff.

Quiet, Still, Alone

Getting alone and shutting off the world has become an almost lost art! Spending quality time alone — especially in the early morning hours, should be a requisite for daily living.

Listen. After you have gotten still and quiet — total silence — you have conditioned yourself to hear God speak. And speak He does! In thoughts, words, images, feelings, in ways that perhaps only you can understand.

You must trust that what you are hearing — especially when what you hear is spoken in a tender, loving and caring way — that this is God. It's like when a dog, or pet, hears his master speak, he knows he is spoken to!

But you are more than some family pet! You are an offspring of God — created with the natural ability to hear and understand the voice of your Maker.

You will hear the voice of God *within*! Nowhere in this book have I said anything about hearing an audible voice, heard by the outward physical ear! It's *within* you, where the spirit-world exists — that's where you and God walk and talk together!

Now sometimes God speaks so deep inside you that his voice overrides the other sounds that surround you. That is God intervening when we mess up! But I think for the most part we have to get still and alone — not for God to speak, but for us to listen!

You must shut out everything, even wandering thoughts, unless even there it is the Spirit doing the wandering. Total quietness is hard to find in our day of hustle and bustle. It seems like we are in a hurry to get nowhere — and when we get there we can't wait to go again!

Nearly every time Edna and I travel a distance of hundreds of miles to arrive at a certain destination, after we have been there 30 minutes to an hour, she wants to go again! What to know where? Wal-Mart!! (I can see that I have quit preaching and gone to meddling!)

Find yourself submerged in God's house — nature! You may live in an urban concrete jungle and have to visualize or create a place in your imagination. You are really blessed if you can actually physically go to the mountains, the woods, the hills, a river or stream, or an ocean! Remember, when God made man He did not put him in a shopping center, but in a garden!

When you get there, not only turn the radio off, but shut down the engine. Take time ... precious time ... quality time ... an hour or two ... a whole day ... maybe several days. Take whatever you need and do not get in a hurry! I'm preaching to myself as much as I am to you!

Now relax! Unwind. Take a nap! Just listen! Listen to what surrounds you — the wind blowing through the trees, the water flowing gently over the rocks, the birds singing. Get quiet. Really quiet! Just LISTEN!

Postscript

This book was written during a three week trip in our motorhome up the Blue Ridge Parkway through North Carolina and Virginia, up through the West Virginia towns of Princeton, Beckley, Charleston, and Hurricane, and into Mt. Vernon and Berlin, Ohio. It was completed in the heart of Amish Country at an R.V. park in Berlin, Holmes County, the largest population of Amish in America at 48,000. It has been a *successful* trip!

— O.C.P.

Key vocabulary words in my new theology

∽

I have noticed several new words in my overall vocabulary gained over the past decade or so. They are so prominent with me that I placed them on plastic pigs on a 50' fence on the front of our parking lot at the BAR-B-Q. This is called "Doc Hopper's PIG-ette fence!" I did this for a conversation piece to remind me every time I drive into the parking lot, and I am ready for that media person to show up with his camera and ask me to explain what "these pigs" mean! Remember, I said earlier that our business represents a new forum from which to share my views. I know that's going to happen! So when it does it won't be a surprise, and I'll be ready.

And, don't forget that our pigs are "spiritual pigs!" The have been "through the fire — and delivered from the pit!"

The following list is taken from the fence. This is only a partial listing of my beliefs, but they are representative!

Presence	Space-Time-	Exponential
Connections	Matter-Motion	New
Change	Partakers	As If
Words	Thoughts	Receiving
Success	Idea	Goals
Imagery	As-He-is	Expansive
Spirit	Emanations	Manifest
Constant	Auras	CBA
Speak-To-It	Process	Direction
Relationships	Christ	Genius
Be-GENES	Love	Affirmation
Re-GENES	I Am	Potential
Joy	Openness	Wisdom
Within	Now	Understanding
Unity	Let	See
Imagine	Relevant	
Conceive	Music	
Believe	Eternally Present	
Achieve	Faith	
Can Do	Holistic	
Listen — Hear	Focus	
Knowledge	Uni-Verse	
I — Thou	Emerging	
Leadership	Calling Things	
Eclectic	Good	
Vision	Self-Image	

Made in the USA
Charleston, SC
24 August 2010